ELIZABE

MAGGIE CARPENTER

CHIMERA

Elizabeth's Education first published in 2003 by
Chimera Publishing Ltd
22b Picton House
Hussar Court
Waterlooville
Hants
PO7 7SQ

Printed and bound in Great Britain by
Cox & Wyman Ltd, Reading.

ELIZABETH'S EDUCATION

Maggie Carpenter

This novel is fiction – in real life practice safe sex

'As I said, I am going to sit on that chair, and then lay you across my lap, face down. I'm going to lift your dress above your waist, and your petticoat as well. Then I am going to pull your drawers down, exposing your bare bottom.'

Elizabeth felt her face turn scarlet and her eyes grew wider still.

'And do you know what I'm going to do then, Elizabeth?' he asked mildly, and she shook her head from side to side, terrified of what he was about to say. 'Well, then I'm going to spank you, Elizabeth, with the lovely gardens as a delightful backdrop. And when my hand gets tired, my dear, do you know what I'll do then?'

Elizabeth gasped through the gag in apprehensive disbelief.

'I asked you a question, Elizabeth,' he said firmly. 'Answer me. Do you know what I'll do when my hand is tired?'

Utterly befuddled and overcome, Elizabeth shook her head again.

'I will take off one of my shoes, and spank you with the sole of that. I think, for the first lesson of the day, that should do very nicely. Now then, young lady, your true education is about to begin.'

Chapter One

It was late, and tucked up in her four-poster bed, her hair carefully pinned, Elizabeth closed her eyes and replayed the events of the day.

Lord Michael had come to the manor, and despite her feverish attempts to get his attention he paid her no heed whatsoever. Instead he had gone shooting with her annoying older brother, James, and then spent the entire evening smoking cigars and drinking brandy with her father in the drawing room.

'It is not a place for young ladies,' her father had told her more often than she cared to remember, and so she was banished from their company after dinner. Exiled. Men and their rules, and their stinky old habits!

She just did not understand it, for her charms were near legendary. All the eligible young men, and even the majority of the older ones, married or no, were eager to spend time with her. At all the balls and events she attended her dance card was always full, and while she thoroughly enjoyed the attention bestowed upon her at these gatherings, she could not help but feel a little frustrated that the enigmatic Lord Michael had never once joined the admiring throngs.

Before the last such event, she had insisted upon travelling into London to buy a brand new gown. She was determined to look ravishing, and though she would not admit it to anyone but herself, she wanted to look ravishingly irresistible for him!

She found a dress that was the newest fashion from Paris. It was a deep blue satin, and in the latest style was tight about her waist and fit snugly over her hips. The bodice was trimmed in fine lace and boasted a high collar, accentuating her slender throat. The seamstress had cleverly sewn sequins here and there, haphazardly, which shimmered in the light.

When Grace, her maid, had finished pinning Elizabeth's hair on top of her head, a twinkling sapphire comb to one side, she was very pleased with her appearance. She stood in front of her full-length mirror admiring the overall picture. As far as she was concerned, Lord Michael must surely take notice now.

But no, on the contrary, he did not. In fact, he did not even stay at the party very long, and it seemed to her that every time she glanced in his direction he was looking decidedly bored, and even once she caught him surreptitiously shielding a yawn of tedium behind a hand.

So when she heard her father had invited him for the coming weekend she was delighted. Given the close proximity that would now be theirs, she was sure he would fall madly in love with her, as had all the other men that crossed her path.

But even during dinner, when she made sure she was placed next to him, all she saw was the back of his shoulder. He carried on an endless, and what seemed to her to be an incredibly tedious conversation, about the latest developments in the import and export trade, with the older gentleman seated to his left.

Who cared where the silks came from, as long as they were pretty and soft? As long as they ended up encasing her lithesome body in the latest fashions, what did it matter the cost of tariffs and such? Men could be such bores.

Yet she sensed something in his indifference. It seemed to be calculated rather than simple disinterest. Had it been her imagination, or had she seen him glance at her that afternoon, as she sat sipping tea in the garden?

He had been trudging up the rear lawns with her brother, guns slung over their shoulders, the hounds barking and running beside them. She was sitting alone, and when she turned to look at them she could have sworn he was staring right at her. But it was only fleeting; she may have been mistaken.

Then there were his boots! After their shoot they were the muddiest boots she had ever seen. Smithy, the footman, would have fun getting those off his feet, let alone clean again, she had thought.

When she finished her afternoon tea, and was sure no one was looking, she had secretly gone to the back door, opened it quietly, and peered in at those muddy boots of his. They were black and hefty, the kind of boots a true adventurer would own. They were encased in crusty mud, waiting to be cleaned. Then she sighed, glad it would not be her job to do such a thing. A girl of her station getting her dainty hands all dirty? Good heavens, no! That would never do!

The sound of the bedroom door opening startled her, breaking her reverie. It was Grace, though why she was called Grace was beyond Elizabeth. To her eyes grace was a quality the girl most certainly did not possess. If she were any clumsier the girl would have to carry around a mop and bucket twenty-four hours a day.

'What is it?' she asked impatiently, wanting to return to her thoughts of the day, and Lord Michael. The *mysterious* Lord Michael.

'Sorry to disturb you, Miss Elizabeth,' said the maid. 'I

just wanted to make sure you didn't need anything before I went to bed.'

'No, nothing,' she replied, waving the girl away with a flick of her hand.

Grace curtsied, somewhat red-faced. She knew if she hadn't checked in with her mistress she would surely have been scolded for it the next day, but now she sensed she was in trouble for disturbing her. She sighed. There was certainly no winning with Miss Elizabeth.

Elizabeth snuggled more deeply under the covers. She wished she'd had a bath before retiring. Bother! Grace should have drawn one for her, irrespective of whether she'd asked her to or not. She would have to counsel her in the morning. Yes, a bath was to be waiting for her and it was for the maid to anticipate when it was to be so, and if she didn't want one, so be it. At least it would be ready, just in case.

She also had to remind Grace to bring some more oil of jasmine. She was running low, and she certainly wasn't about to take an unscented bath.

Elizabeth closed her eyes. The sheets were cool and comfortable. She insisted they be changed every three days. She let her head sink into the soft feather pillows, and let her mind revisit the dashing Lord Michael.

Tall, but not too tall, and he stood so straight and handsome, brimming with confidence and surety. Hmmm. She had allowed one or two suitors to kiss her when she felt so inclined, but they were generally such bumblers. She could only imagine what it would feel like to be swept up in the arms of Lord Michael.

She willed herself to sleep, then suddenly realised she had failed to dim the lamp by the door.

'Bother!' she cursed again, angrily. 'Bother, bother, bother! I'm all comfortable and cosy now. I don't want to get out of bed.'

She reached over, pulling a cord hanging at the side of her bed.

Upstairs, in a room not much bigger than Elizabeth's bed, a copper bell jangled above Grace's head. She had just finished saying her nightly prayers, and was in her plain cotton nightdress, but the bell summoning her meant she had to quickly change back into her black dress and white apron, and fix her cap. She would never dare let herself be seen otherwise attired.

Hurriedly she did so, not wanting to keep Miss Elizabeth waiting, fearful of the temper she possessed when kept waiting. Once changed, she ran down the narrow staircase.

'What kept you so long?' Elizabeth demanded irritably, as Grace gingerly opened the door.

'Sorry, Miss Elizabeth, I was already dressed for bed,' the maid said humbly.

'All right, all right,' she snapped testily. 'Turn out the light by the door, and in the morning remind me to tell you about my new bath routine.'

'Yes, miss.'

Grace wasn't surprised her mistress had called her back down for such a small matter. She was used to Elizabeth's spoiled and arrogant manner, and suffered it because she was desperate for the employment. She extinguished the light, and quietly left the darkened room.

As Elizabeth settled down again, eyes closed, pictures of the dashing Lord Michael played in her head, she imagined herself dressed in the finest of clothes, on Lord Michael's arm, attending splendid society parties in

9

London, everyone oohing and aahing over what a truly splendid couple they made. The love shining from his eyes as he looked at her, kissing her hand every time he went to get her yet another glass of champagne, more than willing to be at her beck and call…

Something's wrong, a voice in her dreamy head warned, but she let it go, drifting off, filled with visions of what she was sure would be her happy ending.

Chapter Two

The following morning, after a full and peaceful night's sleep, Elizabeth studied herself in the mirror. There was a soft glow to her complexion, her green eyes were sparkling with mischief and merriment, and she was full of expectation. For some reason she was sure that at some point during the weekend she would find herself in Lord Michael's embrace for the first time, her breasts rising and falling with the insistent, passionate pounding of her heart.

She had selected a pretty pink dress. It emphasised her shapely figure, and highlighted the perfection of her lily-white skin. She had Grace brush her hair until it was smooth and shining lustrously, and style it in a loose, casual manner. The natural curl caused it to cascade around her shoulders. With a hint of rouge on her cheeks and lips, she was as attractive as she could possibly be.

She pulled on a pair of dainty pink shoes that peeked out cheekily from the hem of her dress, allowing just the smallest amount of white stocking to show, and with a last look in the mirror she felt ready to face the day, and the unfathomable Lord Michael.

As she moved to leave her bedroom Grace interrupted her thoughts. 'You wanted to tell me something about your bath, miss?' she prompted, clearly relieved that her young mistress was in such a good mood.

'Oh, yes, see me in the sitting room after breakfast,' Elizabeth said, and glided out of the room and down the stairs, hearing the sound of Lord Michael's dulcet tones in the dining room, and what she overheard both surprised and delighted her.

'Yes, yes. It is a jolly shame. Still, it cannot be helped.'

It was her father. She paused, waiting to hear more. The naughty side of her loved eavesdropping. She had overheard all sorts of juicy things by being quiet and careful.

'I'm very grateful to you sir, what with her mother away,' her father was continuing. 'She's quite a handful, that young lady, quite a handful indeed. From my experience it's best not to leave her alone here. Especially with all the chaps that are want to drop by. I am very grateful to you for staying, I must say. Very grateful indeed.'

She could just imagine her father, twirling the ends of his great moustache. She loved him dearly, but the poor man didn't have a clue. He was so easy to twist around her manipulative finger. She could usually get what she wanted from him just by lowering her head and allowing a single tear to trickle down her cheek. She giggled a little, amused by her own cleverness.

'Is that you, my dear?'

Darn! He had heard her.

'Yes, father,' she called in her sweetest, most musical voice. She continued down the stairs and entered the dining room.

'Good morning everyone,' she said gaily, flashing Lord Michael her cheeriest smile. He nodded to her, a slight curl raising the corners of his mouth, although it was barely a smile at all, and he went immediately back to eating his breakfast.

She pretended not to notice his aloof manner, and

addressed her father again. 'Did I hear you say something, father, about chaps dropping by?' she said, waving her hand, hoping the words would not be lost on Lord Michael. 'I honestly don't know what to do with all these admirers I seem to have acquired.'

'Yes, yes,' he blustered. 'Well I'm afraid something's come up in London, my dear, and James and I must attend to it at once. So as your mother's visiting your aunt I have asked Lord Michael to stay here, to keep an eye on things for me. I don't feel comfortable leaving you alone here, but we'll be back late tomorrow afternoon and in the meantime you'll be in safe hands.'

She suppressed a squeal of joy, but managed to say, very coolly indeed, she thought, 'How kind of you to put yourself out so, Lord Michael. I shall do my best to make sure you are properly and suitably entertained. Though I shan't be trudging across muddy fields with you, like silly old James would.'

Her brother glowered at her. 'Really, Elizabeth,' he responded irritably. 'We're sportsmen. You couldn't possibly understand.'

'No, I couldn't, nor would I want to, so there,' she countered. 'I don't see any fun in getting all dirty. I will find much finer and more dignified ways to entertain our esteemed guest.'

She looked over at Lord Michael, and to her shock he looked right back at her, an eyebrow arched in what she thought was quite a suggestive manner – though suggestive of what, she had absolutely no idea.

'We shall see who entertains who, and how, won't we Elizabeth?' he stated confidently, and she felt herself blushing, immediately looking away.

'I say,' James chuckled, 'it looks like you might have

met your match there, Elizabeth.'

'Oh, James,' she scoffed, gathering her wits again. 'You don't know what you're talking about. I'm sure Lord Michael means that he intends to entertain me, in return for my entertaining him. Isn't that so, Lord Michael?'

'Yes, Elizabeth,' he said quietly but firmly, 'that is exactly what I mean.'

'We really must be going if we plan to be in London before lunch,' her father said, ignoring the trivial spat between his offspring; he had long since learned to pay no heed to such things. 'Thank you again, my dear friend,' he said to the assured gentleman. 'I am in your debt, sir.'

'My pleasure, I'm sure,' Lord Michael said smoothly. 'I will see you tomorrow. Do not worry about a thing. Your dutiful daughter will be well taken care of.'

Something in the tone of his voice made Elizabeth feel uneasy as her father and brother rose from the table, leaving the two of them alone. There absence for a day was much, much more than she could ever have hoped for, but as they proceeded to finish breakfast the atmosphere was strained. Lord Michael's monosyllabic responses to Elizabeth's attempts at conversation were frustrating her, to say the least, and she was relieved when the meal came to an end.

She excused herself and disappeared into the sitting room. She needed to compose herself. He was certainly most different to any man she had ever encountered. Normally such indifferent behaviour would see her put the gentleman directly in his place, but Lord Michael had the unmistakable aura of someone not to be trifled with.

Then she heard her name being called; her father and brother were about to leave, so she hurried out to the front porch and found herself standing next to Lord

14

Michael, waving goodbye to dear old pater and her bothersome brother. Whilst she couldn't have been happier with the prospect of spending the next thirty-six hours with Lord Michael, she couldn't ignore the sense of uncertain discomfort permeating her being.

She and her handsome guest walked slowly back into the house, and she was trying to think of something witty and smart to say when Grace appeared.

'You want to see me in the sitting room now, miss?' she asked reverently.

'Yes, I'll be along shortly,' Elizabeth replied, rather abruptly. 'Go and wait for me there.'

'Yes, miss,' Grace replied, then curtsied.

'What a charming girl,' Lord Michael said admiringly as she walked away. 'So polite and well mannered. As a young woman should be, don't you think?' He stared into Elizabeth's eyes, once again causing a deep red blush to rise in her cheeks.

'It's only because I've trained her so well,' Elizabeth stated haughtily, attempting to ignore the fact that she was continuing to redden under his unwavering gaze.

'All young ladies need training,' he said, still staring at her intently.

Elizabeth couldn't bring herself to look back at him. She could feel his eyes boring through her. 'Well, I'm about to do some instruction,' she managed. 'So if you will excuse me?'

'Actually, I think I'll join you,' he said. 'You don't have any objection, I take it?'

'Um, no, if you wish. It will only take a minute or two.'

She walked ahead of him into the sitting room, the slim cut of her dress accentuating the sway of her shapely hips and bottom. She could feel his eyes upon her as she moved, and suddenly wished she was walking beside him, rather than in front. She quickened her pace, hurrying to get out of the uncomfortable situation, and as soon as she entered the sitting room she stood with her back to the fireplace.

Grace was standing demurely in the centre of the room, hands clasped in front of her, staring at the floor. She was obviously very uncomfortable.

'Now, Grace,' Elizabeth began, 'last night it occurred to me that I wanted a bath.'

'Yes, miss,' Grace said, clearly unsure of what she had done wrong this time.

'Don't speak until I say you may, you rude girl,' Elizabeth snapped, 'just listen to me.'

'Sorry, miss, I try to do things right,' Grace blurted. 'Honest I do.'

'Be quiet and let me finish!' she snapped again. 'From now on, every night, you must draw my bath whether or not I tell you to. Can you understand that simple instruction?'

'Yes, miss,' the maid answered, visibly cowering, her voice tremulous.

'Well thank goodness for that. And make sure there's plenty of scented oil. I checked this morning and you've allowed my supply to dwindle. Now then, tell me what you're to do in future, beginning with this very evening.'

'I'm to draw your bath every night, whether or not you tell me to,' Grace said, a small sob escaping her lips, 'and make sure there's plenty of oil of jasmine, or milk of roses, or scented oil of some kind, for you, miss.'

'Excuse me.' Lord Michael's voice startled them both, interrupting Elizabeth's flow. 'Surely that's a bit extravagant? All that water possibly going to waste, and the cost of heating it? I'm sure your father would not approve of such a wasteful habit. It's one thing if you decide you want a bath, but to have Grace draw you one just in case, well now, Elizabeth, I do not think that's acceptable. No, not acceptable at all.'

Elizabeth's face began to turn red again, but this time with simmering anger. 'Lord Michael,' she said resolutely, 'forgive me, but this does not concern you.'

'Actually,' he calmly countered, moving to the centre of the room, giving the impression of supporting Grace, 'your father asked me to keep an eye on things here, and my eyes do not approve of what they are seeing.'

Grace's mouth fell open; never had she seen Miss Elizabeth spoken to in such a manner.

'Well, in that case your eyes can just look at something else, because this is how I want it, and this is how it's going to be!' Elizabeth spat, in complete disbelief that the man of her dreams would address her so.

'Grace,' said Lord Michael, ignoring Elizabeth's outraged response, 'I suspect you work very hard here, do you not?'

Grace realised her mouth was still open, and closed it, casting her eyes down. 'I do my best, sir, yes,' she replied.

'I am sure you do,' he said compassionately. 'Now, I have a question for you, and when I ask you this question you must promise to answer truthfully.'

'Yes, sir, I always tell the truth,' she replied, daring to look up at him, a scrap of confidence returning.

'Excuse me,' Elizabeth interjected indignantly, 'but if you don't mind, this is my house! What do you think you're doing?'

'Noisy, isn't she?' said Lord Michael, winking at Grace.

Elizabeth was furious, and the way he was ignoring

17

her, talking about her rather than to her – and to one of the staff, to boot – was making her even more furious by the second. And then to have the audacity to call her noisy!

'I am going to whisper the question in your ear,' he went on to the maid. 'Is that all right, my dear?'

Grace looked up into his eyes, and saw kindness and strength there. 'Yes, sir,' she said quietly. 'Of course, sir.'

Then Elizabeth watched in horror as Lord Michael leaned closer and whispered something to the maid, and Grace broke into a broad grin and then laughed out loud!

'Oh, Lord Michael, no sir,' the servant girl giggled. 'Never. I think I'd die from shock.'

'Fine, Grace,' he said, smiling at her. 'That's what I thought. You may take the rest of the day off. Your mistress will not be needing you. Have a lovely time, and return to your duties promptly tomorrow morning.'

'You'll do no such thing!' Elizabeth exclaimed heatedly, but Lord Michael merely took Grace gently by the arm, guiding her to the door.

'Thank you ever so much, sir,' she said, clearly amazed at this turn of events, clearly confident that she would be all right as long as she did as Lord Michael said.

He smiled at her kindly, and closed the door behind her.

'How dare you?' Elizabeth demanded, stamping her foot in fury.

'Elizabeth,' he said calmly, ignoring her tantrum, 'would you like to know what I asked Grace?'

She hadn't expected a question in response to her indignation, and it caught her off guard.

'Elizabeth?' he prompted, his tone insistent.

'I couldn't care what you asked her,' she spat back at him. 'You have no right to interfere with how I utilise my staff.'

'I asked her,' Lord Michael continued, easily, 'if you ever said please or thank you. And you heard her response, didn't you?'

'She's my servant, and I shall treat her as I please,' she stated vehemently.

Lord Michael crossed his arms and frowned, then after a moment he clasped his hands behind his back and wandered about the room, ending up at the desk by the bay windows, overlooking the landscaped gardens.

'What staff is here today?' he asked, staring out at the view.

'Excuse me?' Elizabeth replied, genuinely perplexed by the odd question.

'Are you deaf?' he said sharply, making her jump slightly. 'What staff is here today?'

'Everybody's off today except the cook and Smithy, the footman,' she answered, still wondering why he would care.

'Wasn't that Smithy I saw, driving the cab for your father?'

'Oh, yes it was,' she acknowledged. 'The usual driver has the weekend off. Only cook, then. Downstairs.

'Excellent,' he mused, his eyes still scanning the lovely grounds, and Elizabeth realised she was being distracted. Was that what the questions were about? Just to get her mind off his interference?

'Now look here, Lord Michael,' she said. 'What's the point of all this? I want to talk about Grace—'

'Elizabeth, you really are a very spoiled and ill-mannered young lady, aren't you?'

'I beg your pardon?' she gasped in shock. 'Oh, you... you...' she blustered, trying to think desperately of an

19

appropriate response.

'Now, the thing is, Elizabeth,' he continued, ignoring her childish protestations, 'I do not think it's entirely your fault. You've not received the proper education for a young female of your means and bearing.'

He moved closer to the oak desk and carefully pulled out the armless desk chair. It was straight-backed with a wide, beautifully padded seat, upholstered in burgundy velvet. He placed it facing the windows.

'Lord Michael,' she replied, shaking with rage, 'I have been very well educated indeed, thank you. I have even attended a finishing school in Paris. How dare you suggest such a thing? You don't know what you're talking about, so I would thank you to mind your own—'

'That's not exactly the education I was referring to,' he said, cutting her short, standing next to the chair. 'Come here, young lady.' His tone and demeanour were unwavering, not to be argued with, and she found herself almost mesmerised by them. But no, she thought determinedly, she would not do as he said.

'I am quite happy here, thank you,' she replied loftily, raising her chin, 'and I wish to discuss this matter about Grace. It needs to be sorted—'

Again he prevented her from making her point. 'It would be wise to do as I say,' he warned ominously, and a voice in her head told her to move, but her stubbornness won out. She stood perfectly still, challenging him.

'Oh dear,' Lord Michael sighed. 'Very well, if you must behave as you do, then I suppose you must. I suppose I shouldn't be surprised.'

The pace with which he moved across the room shocked her, like a striking snake, but what shocked her even more was the ease with which he grabbed her by the wrists with one hand, produced a long piece of black satin from his pocket with the other, and in seconds had both her wrists crossed and bound together.

'Lord Michael,' she gasped, 'what on earth do you think you're doing?'

'You continue to be noisy, don't you?' he said. 'So I'm afraid we're going to have to do something about that.'

Elizabeth launched into a tirade of insults and protests, which he calmly ignored whilst pulling a crisp white handkerchief from his breast pocket, and then the ascot from around his neck. 'Now then,' he said assertively, 'this should shut you up.'

'What?' she wailed, but with deft timing the handkerchief was stuffed into her open mouth, and he spun her round and placed the longer ascot scarf across the gag and tied it behind her head, amused by her now muffled protests.

'And although we are fairly well alone, just to make sure we are not caught unawares and interrupted by someone unexpectedly…' he said, moving quickly to lock the door.

He turned sharply and returned to where she stood, shocked and staring at him over the gag with wide, bewildered eyes. With one arm he picked her up by the waist, lifting her easily, and carried her to the waiting chair.

'It would have been much easier if you had just come to me when I said,' he stated as he stood her back down, and unable to answer, Elizabeth stamped her feet, letting out a muffled screech.

'Be quiet at once!' he barked. 'If you stamp those feet again I'll tie your ankles together as well!'

Though frustrated and angry, not to mention a bit scared and bemused, Elizabeth suddenly realised Lord Michael

21

was to be listened to. At least at this juncture, so she stood still.

'That's better,' he went on, speaking in a stern but quieter voice. 'Now then, I'm going to tell you exactly what I intend to do with you. First, until I know you won't talk back or question me in any way, the handkerchief is going to remain in your mouth. If I take it out and you misbehave, it will go back in immediately. Nod your head if you understand me.'

Elizabeth stared at him in stunned astonishment. She made a funny sound and Lord Michael frowned. He reached down and lifted her skirt and she let out a muffled squeal and recoiled, stepping sideways. But he grabbed her arm, yanking her back.

'Stand still!' he commanded, his eyes penetrating hers.

Once again he lifted the skirt, holding it up with one hand. With the other he slapped the side of her stockinged thigh, hard, making her squeal through the gag and wince.

'I asked you a simple question,' he continued. 'When I ask you a question, simple or otherwise, you will answer me immediately. If you do not you will be punished. Now, do you understand what I said about the handkerchief? Nod if you understand. Shake your head if you do not.'

Once again his tone was controlled, calm, not angry at all, and she nodded her head furiously, her slightly dishevelled locks spilling around her face.

'Good,' he said with satisfaction. 'Now, I am going to sit on that chair. Look at it, Elizabeth. Look at the chair.'

She didn't really understand why he wanted to her stare at the desk chair, but she did as he ordered, the sting in her thigh suggesting strongly that she obey.

'As I said, I am going to sit on that chair, and then lay you across my lap, face down. I'm going to lift your dress above your waist, and your petticoat as well. Then I am going to pull your drawers down, exposing your bare bottom.'

Elizabeth felt her face turn scarlet and her eyes grew wider still.

'And do you know what I'm going to do then, Elizabeth?' he asked mildly, and she shook her head from side to side, terrified of what he was about to say. 'Well, then I'm going to spank you, Elizabeth, with the lovely gardens as a delightful backdrop. And when my hand gets tired, my dear, do you know what I'll do then?'

Elizabeth gasped through the gag in apprehensive disbelief.

'I asked you a question, Elizabeth,' he said firmly. 'Answer me. Do you know what I'll do when my hand is tired?'

Utterly befuddled and overcome, Elizabeth shook her head again.

'I will take off one of my shoes, and spank you with the sole of that. I think, for the first lesson of the day, that should do very nicely. Now then, young lady, your true education is about to begin.'

Chapter Three

Try as she might Elizabeth was no match for Lord Michael, and within seconds of his lecture she was indeed stretched across his lap. He balanced her perfectly, her feet and hands just touching the floor, and held her securely by the waist waiting for her endearing struggles to cease. He knew she would tire quickly, a few minutes passed, and then her wriggles began to subside.

'Really, Elizabeth,' he scolded, 'that was quite a demonstration, and for that you must also be punished. From now on, when you require discipline you will lift your own skirt and petticoat, lower your own panties, then place yourself across my lap for your spanking.'

She couldn't imagine such a thing, and she never intended being in such a situation ever again!

He reached down and slowly lifted the hem of her dress. As it passed over her thighs she cringed, mortified at the pending exposure. Slowly he pulled on the fabric, sliding it over her hips, causing her to release a muffled squeal. When he had trailed it up past her waist he folded the material under itself, so it would not slip back down.

Lord Michael stared at the rounded contours nestled beneath the satin petticoat. He placed his hand on the smooth fabric, letting it rest there, and Elizabeth felt her face burn.

'Feel this hand?' he said. 'Think about it, Elizabeth. In just a minute I will be laying it upon your bare bottom with stinging smacks. And whilst I'm doing so I want you to think about why I am spanking you. Do you understand?'

The feel of his hand on her virgin cheek, even though it was through fabric, dominated Elizabeth's thoughts, and it was all she could focus on. Then the warmth of his hand was gone.

He smacked her hard on the back of her thigh, saving her bottom until it was naked. Her head jerked up and she let out a muffled wail.

'I asked you a question, you rude girl,' he said sternly. 'Answer me!'

She tried to remember what the question was, but she couldn't. All she could think about was the sharp stinging in her thigh, and the heat of the embarrassment surging through her.

'Elizabeth,' said Lord Michael, sensing her confusion, placing his hand back upon her tingling buttock, 'you must pay strict attention. When I speak, regardless of the circumstances, you must be listening intently. Do you understand?' He trailed his hand to the bright pink spot on her thigh and her head bobbed up and down. 'Good. You are to think about why you are being spanked. Do you understand?' He squeezed the area of the slap and felt her wince. She vigorously bobbed her head again. 'Very well, then we shall continue.'

Elizabeth felt her petticoat being drawn up, and was mortified that at any moment she would be laying with just a single layer of fine silk covering her nakedness. Oh, what had she done to him to deserve such mortifying treatment? Why was he being such a brutish beast?

She felt his fingers play with the tie around the top of her most private of undergarments, and thought she would die of humiliation. Using both hands he undid the bow, then let his fingernails lightly scrape the fine skin of her cheeks as he slowly pulled the panties down. She gasped in horror, her face burning with embarrassment.

Soon the flimsy silk underwear was dangling unevenly from her thighs, just above her knees. Lord Michael smiled; her clothing was in disarray, but she looked exquisitely attractive nonetheless. He feasted his eyes upon her splendid derrière. So delicious was it, it just begged to be spanked, so white and virginal. He caressed the skin with his hands, pinching lightly, watching the blood come and go. It would please him indeed to witness the white flesh turning crimson under his discipline. The rudeness with which she treated those unfortunate enough to have been born below her station was cause for discipline alone. Not to mention her lofty airs and graces. Oh, she was going to be spanked for certain, as she should have been many times before.

Though horrified at her forced nakedness, Elizabeth was being strangely calmed by the soft caresses of his hand upon her smooth skin. She also felt a peculiar excitement moving through her nether regions, and began to breathe a little easier. Perhaps it had all been a big bluff…

But to her astonishment and dismay his hand suddenly swept down, twice, landing with fire. She kicked out, the hot sting sparking through her like an electric shock. He had spanked her on each cheek with significant force, and her involuntary scream sounded odd through the gag. She waited, breathing heavily through flared nostrils, tense.

'Those were just the first two of many, Elizabeth,' Lord Michael said severely. 'You'd better relax your body or you'll be totally exhausted when we're done, and you have a long day ahead of you. I won't allow you to slack off for one minute either, young lady. Now calm your breathing.'

Attempting to do as he said she took several deep breaths, in an attempt to compose herself as much as the circumstances would allow. His hand landed again and she gasped, and then his open palm continued to rise and fall on her tender flesh.

Lord Michael observed with satisfaction as the spanking caused a deepening red glow to spread across her deliciously round bottom.

'You are a rude, thoughtless, petulant, and arrogant young lady,' he said as he continued to spank her, 'and you are totally without humility.'

Elizabeth couldn't believe this was happening to her as her muffled cries kept pace with his smacking hand. His words stung almost as much as his slaps.

'You are disobedient,' he went on, 'and you are disrespectful. Not to mention wasteful and wilful. And you treat the servants poorly.'

She twisted and wriggled but he held her securely, never missing a beat. Soon tears were squeezing from her tightly shut eyes, and with each smack she felt the sting more acutely. Then just when she was sure she could take no more, the punishment stopped. Her heart was pounding, her breathing ragged.

Lord Michael gazed out at the picturesque garden. The early-autumn sun was casting its mid-morning glory across the lush green lawns. The spoiled girl was attempting to regain some kind of control, so he waited until her writhing became less so, and when finally he felt she could pay him attention, he cast his eyes back down upon her ruby-red bottom.

'Now Elizabeth, pay attention,' he said clearly and precisely. 'I am going to remove your gag, but it is under

27

the following conditions. One, you are not to speak unless spoken to. Two, you will not answer a question with a question. Three, when I resume your spanking you must do your best to stifle your outbursts. If you make too much noise the gag will be replaced. Do you understand me?'

The thought of losing the gag filled Elizabeth with relief, so she nodded her head fervently.

'Good. All right, be still now.'

He reached down and undid the knot nestled in her hair, removing the ascot. He then placed his hand under her mouth and slowly pulled the wet handkerchief from between her lips. Elizabeth could still taste the laundered cotton, but to feel the release of the gag around her head brought great relief.

'Take it in your hands, Elizabeth,' he ordered, 'so you will remember that if you disobey those conditions it will be smartly reinserted.'

Carefully balancing across his lap, she raised her bound hands to take the damp material from him, but he pulled it away and she furrowed her brow, confused.

'Don't you have anything to say?' he demanded, and she thought furiously, trying to understand. 'Aren't you grateful for the removal of the gag, Elizabeth?'

'Y-yes,' she stammered.

'Yes what, Elizabeth?'

'Yes, I am.' What was he driving at now? She didn't understand him at all.

'Wrong answer, Elizabeth.'

His hand smacked again, two more times, helping her remember the edict, and though the smacks hurt terribly she didn't cry out as she wished she could.

'Let's try again,' he persisted. 'Yes, what?'

'Yes, sir,' she replied, feeling foolish and cross that she hadn't thought of it before.

'Good girl,' he said, his voice suddenly gentle as he tenderly stroked her stinging cheeks, and his words, in conjunction with his soothing caress, sent a strange thrill through her, penetrating her sorry state.

'Elizabeth, when one is grateful what does one say?' he pressed, as if addressing a simple child.

She thought for a moment, trying to control her panting, encouraged by his sudden change in demeanour.

'Thank you?' she replied, hopefully.

'Thank you, what?' he asked patiently.

'Thank you, sir,' she answered, finally understanding him now. She was to address him as 'sir' at all times.

'Good girl,' he responded warmly, and offered her the handkerchief.

She accepted the damp gag in trembling hands, so pleased she had gotten it right, and wondered what strange phenomenon was taking place.

'Now, we shall continue,' he said, 'and when I ask certain questions you'll know the correct answers, won't you?'

'Yes, sir,' she replied, suddenly filled with renewed dread of what was to come.

'Are you rude?' he began, the next smack landing on the last word.

'Yes, sir, I am rude,' she cried.

'Thoughtless?' he continued, the palm of his hand underlining the question.

'Yes, sir,' she wailed. 'I am thoughtless.'

'Are you petulant and arrogant, Elizabeth?' he asked, two slaps hitting on each cheek.

'Yes, sir,' she cried, her sobs growing louder.

29

'And disobedient?'

'I am very disobedient, sir,' she sobbed.

'And the bath, Elizabeth, are you wasteful?' His hand landing one more swat on her scarlet skin.

'I *am* wasteful, sir,' she cried. 'Yes, I am wasteful.'

'And how do you treat your servants, Elizabeth?'

'Badly, sir,' she admitted, knowing through the pain and tears it was true.

'Yes, you do, Elizabeth,' he confirmed, landing one more sound slap. 'But you answered all the questions correctly, didn't you? Good girl.'

Once again Elizabeth felt a strange sense of satisfaction at his words, though her flesh was smarting and she was mortified at the turn of events. Then as his hand travelled over her skin she heard him say, 'Think about everything you've just acknowledged, Elizabeth, and what it is I'd like to hear next.'

He listened to her sniffles as he caressed her burning cheeks. With continued training she would become and remain pliable, obedient, and worth the time and attention of a gentleman. And she would have to be spanked regularly; such spirit as hers needed to be kept in check. Then at last he heard the words he'd been waiting for.

'I'm sorry!' she suddenly blurted. 'Please, sir, I'm so sorry!'

He smiled with satisfaction. 'That took you long enough,' he said. 'But perhaps the people you mistreated are the ones who deserve your apologies.'

'Yes, sir,' she replied, happy to agree with anything he might say.

'Starting with Grace. When you see her tomorrow morning you're going to apologise to her, aren't you, Elizabeth?'

The suggestion shocked her, and she hesitated fatefully.

'My hand is quite tingling,' Lord Michael stated, then reached down and pulled off his leather shoe. She couldn't see exactly what he was doing, and for a moment she thought he had been distracted. But then a shockingly sharp pain reverberated through her bottom and she shrieked pitifully.

'That was too loud,' he admonished ruthlessly. 'Do we need the gag again, Elizabeth?'

The terrible sting of the shoe left her breathless, and she shook her head miserably.

'N-no, sir,' she stammered through ragged breaths. 'S-sorry, sir, it won't happen again.'

'I should think not. Now, I asked you a question, Elizabeth, and you didn't answer me so I shall repeat it for you. You're going to apologise to Grace, aren't you?'

'Yes, sir,' she said, her voice wavering, 'I am going to apologise to Grace.'

'Good. And then you will apologise to your father, and your brother, and Smithy. In fact, everyone to whom you have ever been rude. Isn't that right, Elizabeth?'

'Y-yes, s-sir,' she spluttered.

'Excellent.' He smiled contentedly. 'Now, just to even things up, and so you will definitely remember what will happen to you should you decide to disobey me…' The shoe leather hit her other cheek with a scorching slap and she hissed, clenching her teeth, but she did not shriek as she had previously.

'All right, Elizabeth,' he concluded, 'I am going to let you up now. You are to step out of your underwear and you are to keep your garments raised by holding them up under your elbows. Then you will stand by the window until I tell you to move. You may cry, you may sigh, but you may not talk. Do you understand me?'

'Yes, sir,' she said, stifling a sob.

'Good girl. Up you get now.'

He helped her up from his lap, and then stood to steady her as she stepped out of her fine silk drawers, which had been, much to his delight and entertainment, flapping as she helplessly kicked the air during her chastisement. Then obediently holding up her lacy petticoat and skirt, she walked shakily to the window and stood, head bowed, sniffling quietly.

As she studied the floor she knew she had been rude and wilful and unkind to the servants, but as the minutes ticked by the throbbing sting began to abate, she regained her composure, and she found herself wondering if her past behaviour, so unacceptable to Lord Michael, was her right. Wasn't she born to it? It wasn't her fault if she had been blessed by wealth and station. The servants belonged to her family. She may have been unkind from time to time, but they should consider themselves lucky to be even employed!

She wished she was anywhere but there. Suddenly she hated him – sort of. Actually, try as she might it was impossible to hate him, and the truth was she didn't know what she was feeling. Except for the smarting of her bottom and the unexpected wetness between her legs.

She thought about turning and speaking to him, but knew if she did she would be disobeying him, and that was the last thing she wanted to do. He would surely spank her all over again, and she was sore enough, thank you. No, she would stand there as long as he wanted. That would be that, and then she would go to her room and rest for the remainder of the day.

Lord Michael viewed his handiwork. Her bottom was a

lovely blotchy shade of pinks and reds. Undoubtedly she would need some more hearty smacks from him before the day was out, and definitely more in the days and weeks to come, but she was fixable, he was sure of it. She was a very naughty young lady; even more so than he had at first thought. He knew it would take more than one sound spanking to teach her the error of her ways, and he was more than up to the task. Indeed, he was looking forward to the challenge immensely.

Chapter Four

Long after she had stopped sobbing and the scalding pain had turned to a dull throb, Elizabeth was still standing, holding her dress, staring at the floor. She could hear Lord Michael moving about the room, and wanted desperately to speak to him, or to simply drop her dress and walk out.

She was becoming increasingly uncomfortable and her bound wrists were really starting to annoy her. Twice she had an itch on the tip of her nose, but she couldn't reach to scratch it without running the risk of dropping her skirt. The situation was starting to make her angry again, and her lesson in wilfulness was fast being forgotten.

Lord Michael was well aware of this. He knew it was only a matter of time before her spoiled nature would get the better of her and she would utter a petulant word, or drop her skirt, or worse. Then her education would continue.

But he decided to expedite the process. Initially he only had the rest of the day, and there was still much to accomplish. So, addressing her from across the room he announced, 'Elizabeth, I am leaving the room for a minute. You are to stay exactly as and where you are.'

With that he unlocked and opened and closed the door, but rather than leave the room, he quietly moved back and stood by the fireplace. It was a deception, but necessary.

Elizabeth heard the door close, then listened intently.

Her arms were aching from holding up the dress, and she really had taken enough. She listened again, cocking her head to one side. She could race up the stairs and lock herself in her room. He wouldn't be able to get in there. Yes, that's what she would do, and she'd better do it while she had the chance.

A wry smile crossed Lord Michael's lips. He could almost hear her considering all the possibilities and options. It wouldn't be much longer now. The atmosphere in the room grew more tense…

Only a few moments more passed and Elizabeth dropped her skirt, turned, started for the door, and stopped abruptly as she saw him standing by the fireplace, hands behind his back, watching her.

'Going somewhere?' he asked.

She froze, shocked and dismayed, and stared into steely brown eyes.

'So, it appears you are still a disobedient young lady.'

'And you are a cheating beast, sir!' Despite her awful predicament she could not suppress the unwise outburst.

He moved with surprising stealth, grabbed her bound wrists and threw her down into a large armchair. Then nonchalantly he reached down and took off his shoe again. 'Do you have anything to say in your defence?' he asked.

Her heart was hammering and she felt completely furious, but the continuing burning in her bottom and the menacing shoe in his hand were keeping her fury in check. She may have been rebellious, but she wasn't stupid.

'I'd just had enough, that's all,' she began, 'and I thought I'd—'

'Elizabeth, stand up,' he snapped, 'lift your skirt, turn around, and bend over.'

Her eyes grew wide.

'You just admitted you were disobedient because you felt like being so. Do you think that's acceptable behaviour?'

Swallowing hard she studied the carpet, and frantically searched for a rational explanation.

'I asked you a question, Elizabeth,' he persisted. 'Was your behaviour appropriate?'

She sighed, resigned to her fate, and shook her head. 'No, sir,' she said quietly, 'I suppose it was not appropriate.'

'And do you think you should be punished?'

'Yes, sir, I suppose I should be punished.'

'Very good, young lady, perhaps something did sink in after all. Come here, lift your skirt and bend over.'

Standing, head bowed, she did exactly as he instructed. He stood for a moment, staring at the beautiful young lady holding her skirt up, bent over at the waist, waiting for her punishment. It was a most pleasing and satisfying sight. He moved closer and positioned himself so he was facing the opposite direction to her, then wrapped his left arm solidly around her waist, his right hand firmly holding the shoe.

'Do not make one sound, Elizabeth,' he warned. 'Do you understand me? Since this is a lesson in obedience, we'll see just how obedient you can be when you put your mind to it.'

Elizabeth could not believe she was in such an awful predicament again. How could she have been so stupid? If only she had done as she'd been told. He was rubbing the cold sole of the shoe across her right buttock. She clenched her teeth and waited... and waited. She felt the leather leave her tender behind, and assumed the smack would be just another second longer. She cringed, but nothing happened. Then the rubbing commenced again, caressing, moving softly. She couldn't bear it. Why didn't he just spank her and get it over with?

'Do you deserve a punishment, Elizabeth?' he asked, continuing to rub the leather over her skin.

The question made her think about her deliberate act of disobedience. 'Yes, sir,' she answered, hoping she sounded repentant enough.

'Why is that, Elizabeth?'

'Because I disobeyed you, sir.'

'That's correct. Ask me to punish you.'

She winced at the humiliating decree. She actually had to ask to be spanked!

'I'm waiting, Elizabeth.'

'Pluh-please, sir, will you punish me for disobeying you?' she blurted.

'Yes,' he mused, 'I most certainly will.'

Lord Michael swept the shoe down hard and flat against her flesh, still tender from the spanking. She felt the pain considerably, the burning smack loud against her delicate skin, but she made not a sound. He moved the shoe to the other cheek, caressed it for a moment, and then smacked it hard. Again there was not a sound from her lips. He repeated the treatment twice more on each cheek, leaving plenty of time between each strike for the sting to penetrate and absorb.

When finished he removed his anchoring hold from around her waist and ordered her to remain bent at the waist. Then moving around in front of her he offered her the article of punishment.

'Elizabeth, take my shoe and kiss it,' he said, 'and thank me for your castigation.'

Utterly defeated, she took the leather item in her bound

hands and pressed her lips to it. 'Thank you for my punishment, sir,' she sniffled.

'Kneel down,' he instructed, 'elbows on the floor, bottom raised, place the shoe back on my foot, and stay there.'

She did as he said, albeit a little clumsily. Her wrists were still tied and her hands still held the damp handkerchief. When she was done she stayed perfectly still, maintaining her submissive posture.

'Good,' he said, and then just stood there gazing down at her. Though it was only a few minutes to Elizabeth, in the pervading silence it seemed a very long time.

'Stay,' he said softly.

He walked across the room, removed the key from the lock, opened the door, walked out and closed it behind him. Standing in the hall he could feel her complete stillness and obedience within the room. He knew she would not move. He locked the door and went to his room to change.

Lord Michael was gone for about twenty minutes, and just as he knew she would be, when he unlocked and opened the door he was greeted by the sight of his petulant young charge still kneeling, her naked bottom raised, red, and exposed. It was a very satisfying sight.

Upon hearing his return Elizabeth breathed a sigh of relief. Her neck was aching and she was miserable, but she was determined not to move, no matter what.

'Stand up.'

The order was like music to her ears, so still holding her skirt she struggled to her feet. The muscles in her shoulders protested and she found her knees were quite sore, but she didn't complain. In fact she barely noticed the discomfort as she faced him.

'Have you thought about anything since I've been gone,

Elizabeth?' he asked.

'Yes, sir,' she admitted. 'That I wasn't to move.'

He laughed. It was perfect. It was the only thought she should have had. 'What would you like to do now, Elizabeth?' he went on.

'I'd like to lay down for a rest, sir,' she said.

'No, Elizabeth, that's not what you would like to do,' he countered. 'Think about the question.'

She furrowed her brow. What was he talking about now? That was exactly what she wanted to do, and she should know.

'What would you like to do, Elizabeth?' he repeated.

'Have a bath, sir?' she suggested tentatively, trying again.

'Tell me, my dear, do you ever take into consideration the feelings of another?' he asked, raising his eyebrows. 'Perhaps, for example, you would care to consider my position for a change.'

'Oh, yes sir,' was all she could think of to say. 'Of course sir.'

'Do you see how I'm dressed, Elizabeth?'

She looked at his attire. She hadn't really paid it any attention when he first reappeared, but now she realised he was dressed in his sporting gear, freshly polished boots included.

'Let us go, my dear,' he said. 'I would like to take a stroll in the fields, and so we're going to take a stroll in the fields.'

'B-but, what about my underwear?' she stammered.

He paused, silent and stoic, studying her. The gaze was unnerving.

'What about my panties, sir?' she repeated carefully, wondering if perhaps he hadn't heard her the first time.

'Did I say anything about them?' he asked, his voice

tinged with impatience.

'No, sir,' she answered.

'Elizabeth, just how many smacks are you going to need today?' He sighed dramatically, raised his eyebrows, and cast her a very stern look indeed. 'Lift up your dress again,' he said, getting impatient.

'Oh, but?'

'Did I not tell you, quite clearly,' he interrupted her, 'not to speak unless spoken to, and to do exactly as you are told? If I wanted you to put your drawers back on, would I not have instructed you to do so? Now turn around and bend over. Really, Elizabeth, you are becoming quite tiresome.'

She stifled a protestation but did as he ordered, and received a swift smack on each buttock, then once again he stood in front of her, offering his hand. She obediently took it, kissed the palm, and thanked him for her punishment.

'Straighten up,' he ordered, and she did so, looking up at him gingerly. 'All right, Elizabeth, the gag.' With pleading eyes she lifted her bound wrists and opened her hands, offering the crumpled handkerchief. 'Ask me to gag you, Elizabeth, for speaking out of turn.'

'P-please sir, will you gag me for speaking out of turn?' she asked obediently, a sigh of resignation escaping her lips.

'Very well,' he said, 'open up.'

Elizabeth did as she was told, and Lord Michael gently fed the wadded cotton into her mouth, but he did not tie his ascot around her head on this occasion. 'Hold that in your mouth, Elizabeth, until I tell you otherwise. Do you understand?'

She nodded her head, accepting that she was responsible

for keeping the punishment gag in place.

'Right,' he said briskly, 'follow me.' Without looking back he strode from the room, and Elizabeth, handkerchief in her mouth, wrists bound, minus her underwear, dutifully followed.

Chapter Five

The sky was becoming rather overcast, and he walked swiftly across the manicured lawns towards the picturesque rolling fields beyond. Elizabeth, in her dainty pink shoes and long dress, had difficulty keeping pace and had to run every few steps. It was difficult to maintain her balance, the ground beneath her feet being soft and uneven.

They were soon out of sight of the house, heading down a small incline. It was difficult for her, and by the time Lord Michael had reached the bottom in his sturdy boots, Elizabeth had barely made it halfway down. He stopped and looked up after her. She was attempting to hold up her dress with her bound hands, but it was fairly pointless. The hem of her skirt was quite covered with dirt and her shoes, once a lovely shade of pink, were already wet and slightly muddy. But she looked lovely to him. She was doing her best, and the handkerchief in her mouth wasn't helping. Although it would have to stay there a while longer, he thought. He was sure the point had been made, but he wanted to drive it home. At last she reached him, breathing hard, looking quite agitated.

He pointed across the fields to where the woods started. 'That's where we are headed, Elizabeth, to the woodman's cottage for a brief period of peace and quiet together,' he explained. 'It's a bit muddy between here and there, so watch where you're stepping. Come along now.'

He walked off, and once again she fell in behind him.

He slowed his pace a little, because there were quite a few ruts in the ground and he didn't want her spraining an ankle.

It was a good ten minutes to get across the field, and by the time they reached the trees he felt quite invigorated, the adrenalin pumping through his veins from the brisk exercise. Elizabeth, on the other hand, not used to doing much of anything, was breathing quite heavily.

As they made their way under the canopy of trees towards the little cabin there was an alarming clap of thunder and the sound of rain splattering down on the treetops, the frightening sound and the prospect of getting wet spurring her on. The ground was firmer now and she found her second wind, and before either of them had fallen victim to a downpour they were safely inside the crude abode.

The interior was gloomy. There was only one window that allowed any light, and with the darkness of the sky there was little to be let in. However, a fireplace was conveniently stacked and ready for lighting, and while Elizabeth stood, unsure what to do with herself, Lord Michael went about the business of igniting it.

Within minutes a warm and cosy glow fell over the dingy room, and satisfied with his work, he turned and looked at her. She was shivering slightly, the white of the kerchief showing between her red lips. Her skin was pale, cute tendrils of curly dark hair lay across her brow, and her bright green eyes seemed softer than before. The shrew was dissolving.

He walked over to her. 'Open your mouth, Elizabeth,' he said, and she did so immediately. He removed the kerchief, neatly folded it, and despite it being damp, placed it back in his breast pocket. 'Handy if we need it again, but we won't, will we?' he said, staring into her eyes.

'No, sir,' she replied quietly, then added, 'thank you, sir.'

'Good girl.'

The words sent a gentle wave of warmth through her, and for a moment she felt quite faint.

'Give me your hands, Elizabeth,' he continued.

She lifted them and he gently untied her bonds. She looked up at him, rubbing her wrists. 'Thank you, sir,' she said, and he smiled.

The little cabin was sparsely furnished. There was a small cot, a blanket, a table, and a rocking chair. The floor was bare.

'Lay down and rest a minute, Elizabeth,' he said, pointing to the cot.

'Thank you, sir,' she said, truly grateful, and he smiled again.

'Good girl,' he repeated.

She moved slowly over to the cot and sat, wincing a little as her bottom touched down, a reminder of the spanking he had so deftly administered.

'Stretch out and close your eyes,' he said, and to her surprise he removed her muddy shoes, and as she lay down gently covered her with the blanket. 'Now,' he went on, 'I'm going to make the most of the peace and quiet by enjoying my book,' and he drew a small leather-bound novel from his coat pocket.

In a few minutes she was dozing comfortably. He watched the rise and fall of her chest, indicative of her deep, even breathing. He thought her remarkably beautiful, looking so at peace as she rested. Settling into the rocking chair he allowed the fire to entrance him, and the rhythm of the steady rain lulled him; a reassuring sound, and he invited himself to relax too and flicked open the pages of his book.

If strangers had passed by at that moment and peered in through the window, they would have seen a truly tranquil scene. Lovers, they would assume, the gentleman giving the lady the comfort of the cot, both resting after passion's visit.

When Elizabeth awoke he was standing over her.

'Hello, my dear,' he said. 'Did you have a nice nap?'

'Yes, sir,' she replied, stretching her arms above her head.

'And what would you like to do now, young lady?'

The question sounded familiar, and she knew there was a correct response she was supposed to have.

'Elizabeth?' he prompted, and then it came to her.

'What would you like to do, sir?' she asked tentatively, pleased she had remembered.

'Good girl,' he said. 'That's close enough, although the correct answer is, "whatever pleases you, sir".'

'Yes, sir, whatever pleases you, sir.'

'Good girl,' he repeated, and she felt that surge of warmth again. What *was* it?

'The rain has stopped, but there doesn't seem to be any firewood left,' he told her. 'So I want you to go out and find enough to replace that which we've used. You'll have to poke around because it's been raining, and of course wet wood won't do. But don't take too long.'

'Yes, sir,' she said, sitting up. She found her dirty shoes, slipped her feet into them, and headed for the door.

He knew he could trust her, that she would complete her task diligently and return with the firewood. If he were to tell James that his sister was out seeking kindling in the middle of the woods, wearing dirty attire, he would have thought him mad. It was truly gratifying what a little training could accomplish.

Elizabeth trod carefully around the damp floor of the woods, peering under bushes and fallen tree trunks. She found quite a few sticks that were dry enough, and when she chanced upon a particularly large fallen branch she was thrilled. It was almost like a treasure hunt.

As she picked through the brush, scraping her hands and tearing her dress, she considered Lord Michael. A part of her hated him. He was an arrogant brute, but she was beginning to feel ashamed for her habitual authoritarian behaviour. She was tough on poor Grace, and the rest of the staff, for that matter. And her dear father did work very hard to provide for her and her brother, and she had to admit she could be dreadfully wasteful at times.

By the time her arms were full the sun was out again and shining rays of golden light through the trees. Birds had begun to chirp, and the day was returning to a very pleasant one indeed. She trudged back to the cabin, and as she approached she saw Lord Michael waiting at the door.

'Very well done, my dear,' he beamed. 'Bring it in and stack it by the fire.'

'Yes, sir,' she said, walking past him and stooping to neatly stack her load on the tiny dusty hearth.

'Now, Elizabeth,' he went on as she straightened up and turned, emitting a little sigh as she stretched her back, 'I want you to go out again and find me a sturdy birch rod.'

She gasped in shocked surprise and was about to protest, but thought better of it, suppressed any petulant outburst, and hurried out again without one word of rebellion. Was he going to punish her again, with a birch rod? What had she done wrong now?

The thought of fleeing back to the house crossed her mind, but for some inexplicable reason she really didn't want to leave him, although she didn't want to be chastised again either. She found what he had asked for, reluctantly wrenched a stout rod free and slowly trudged back to the cabin, full of dread and with tears blurring her vision.

She went inside and found him standing with his back to the small fireplace, the fire now just smouldering ashes. As she handed him the rod the tears of apprehension began to trickle down her dusty cheeks.

'Thank you, Elizabeth,' he said, taking it from her. 'Why are you so upset?'

She stared at him, puzzled by the question. 'Aren't you going to birch me, sir?' she asked tentatively.

'Why?' he mused. 'Should I? Have you done something to warrant it?'

'No sir,' she replied, still confused.

'Then why would I birch you?' he asked. 'Do you want me to birch you?'

'No sir,' she said hastily.

'I only punish when punishment is deserved, Elizabeth.' He raised the cane a little. 'This is for future use.'

She let out a sigh of relief, fighting the desire to hug him and failing to register his ominous conclusion.

'And now I am absolutely famished,' he continued breezily. 'We shall go back to the house for a late luncheon.' And with that, birch rod in hand, he walked out of the tiny, dingy cabin. She scurried after him, closing the door behind her.

47

The walk back was more treacherous than the one going. The fairly steep field was soggy and slippery from the heavy downpour, and by the time they made it to the house her knees were muddy from her frequent falls. Eventually they reached the steps to the back door, and he turned and looked down at her.

'Hmm, take off your shoes, Elizabeth,' he instructed. 'Smithy's not here, so you'll have to help me off with my boots.'

She let out a little indignant cry. All she wanted to do was go up to her room for a hot bath and change, and now she was faced with this humiliation! But filled with pique and disappointment, she followed him inside.

He settled himself on the wooden bench against the wall, near the door, and she stood facing him. Never having seen Smithy pull off a pair of boots she wasn't sure how it was done.

'Turn around and bend over,' he instructed her, noting her uncertainty. 'I'll place my foot between your legs. You take a hold of the boot, move it back and forth, and pull. It's as simple as that.'

Elizabeth was horrified. 'Sir?' she squeaked, not believing he was asking her to perform such a menial chore.

'Do as I say, Elizabeth,' he said testily.

'But, sir?' she said again, her brow furrowed in puzzlement; she was still a lady, after all. Yes, despite her better judgement she had completed the demeaning job of gathering wood for him, but he couldn't expect this of her, surely.

Suddenly he had her by the wrists, pulling her forward across his lap again, and once again her dress was rucked up and her bottom exposed. He grabbed the birch rod she'd gathered herself and broke it in half. A few short stinging cuts would do the job, and for the purpose at hand a smaller rod was just the ticket.

'Elizabeth,' he began, lightly tapping the stick on her bottom, 'I gave you a direct order.'

The rod hit her across the centre of her backside and she yelped pitifully.

'You will do as you are told,' he warned, bringing the birch down smartly.

'Oh, yes sir!' she wailed. 'I'm sorry, sir.'

Two more cuts landed on each cheek and she squealed miserably with each one.

'Now stand up and get in the position I just described,' he ordered, his voice resolute, all good humour gone. 'You are to pull off my boots.'

'Yes s-sir,' she stammered, rubbing her poor bottom as she stood. With punished flesh smarting she turned around and bent over, lifting her dress to allow his boot between her thighs. She clutched the muddy leather in her grubby hands, cringing as the mud oozed between her fingers, then felt his other foot against her bottom, pushing her as she pulled. The pressure exacerbated the smart of the punishment she had just received, but she continued to pull and heave. Finally the boot gave, coming off with a start and causing her to stumble forward. She managed to halt her staggering progress before she collided with the wall opposite or fell, and then placed the boot to one side. Pouting sulkily, she then retuned to her position and waited for the other foot.

The second boot appeared between her knees and she began the undignified struggle all over again. Once more the sole and heel pressing against her backside caused the throbbing in her buttocks to worsen, and again she struggled and pulled until the boot jerked off. She placed

49

it next to its partner and straightened up, hoping she could now go to her room, have a hot bath, get cleaned up, and restore some pride and poise.

'Now you will clean them, Elizabeth,' he ordered, 'and I want them to be so shiny, so mud free, one would think I had just bought them.'

She opened her mouth to protest, but her eyes fell on the threatening birch in his fist. 'Yes sir,' she said wearily.

'And when you are finished you may go to your room, freshen up, and then have some lunch. You will eat my leftovers in the kitchen, with cook. I will speak to her about it while you're upstairs.'

Eat in the kitchen? With cook? He had to be joking!

Lord Michael watched her expression intently. He knew the thought of eating below stairs was abhorrent to her, but she needed such a lesson in humility. She needed to see that people were people, be they servants or equals.

'I want my boots cleaned and polished properly, Elizabeth,' he concluded. 'Now stop dallying and get to work.'

He walked away without a second look, and sighing with resignation, she poked around for Smithy's cleaning implements. She found them in a small cupboard and started rummaging through all the rags and brushes, and then as she picked at the hardening mud, being careful not to scratch the quality leather, she sighed again, because when she had thought Lord Michael a force to be reckoned with, she had no idea how accurate her assessment would prove to be.

Chapter Six

Lord Michael cleaned up, then made his way to the dining room. He was pleased with his morning's work, but he was suffering from a growing unease.

He had trained many recalcitrant young women in the past, but something about Elizabeth was different. He had felt it from the moment he first saw her at a summer ball, teasing a hapless young admirer, and on several occasions since he had found it difficult to keep his eyes from following her.

Once he was in control of her, he decided, and she became the sweet submissive female she was born to be, she would be just like the others. She was a project, a pleasurable one to be sure, but a diversion nonetheless.

Though he had to admit at the cabin she had looked particularly lovely and he felt something unexpected stirring. Something unfamiliar, making it difficult to suppress his desire to embrace her. It was not a feeling he'd often experienced before.

He brushed the memory aside, refusing to allow it entry, but as he made his way down the stairs he could not disperse it. The little minx was getting under his skin.

He opened the door to the dining room and sat at the long table to enjoy luncheon. Still particularly hungry, he rang the little bell by his placing.

'Here you are, sir,' said cook, bustling in. 'Some lovely oxtail soup, and I'll be bringing you some pâté when you're done with that.'

She was a merry, overweight woman, with a twinkle in her bright blue eyes and a cheery word for everyone. She looked around, clearly puzzled. 'Won't Miss Elizabeth be joining you, sir?' she asked.

'No, cook,' he said, shaking his head, and cook frowned and waited. 'As a matter of fact, I have instructed Miss Elizabeth to dine with you today, in the kitchen,' he explained. 'She's to eat whatever I cannot finish.'

Cook raised her eyebrows in astonishment. 'Oh, I don't know if Miss Elizabeth will be pleased with that arrangement, sir,' she opined. 'Though I'm very happy to have her, it might—'

He held up his hand with an amiable smile on his face, and she stopped speaking immediately. 'It's taken care of, cook. Simply set a place for her. I want you to address her as you would a common girl from the neighbourhood. I simply want to teach her a little humility, that's all. Will you help?'

Cook rocked back her happy round face, and laughed out loud. 'Why sir, I'd be delighted,' she boomed heartily. 'A little humility is just what that little madam needs, if you don't mind my saying so, sir. I'd be happy to do my bit, sir. Very happy indeed. When should I expect her little highness to dine with me?'

She shook a little as she chuckled at her own slightly derisive quip, and Lord Michael smiled warmly. The woman was a gem.

'I suspect in about forty-five minutes or so,' he told her.

'Very well, sir,' she said, winking, 'and I'll be out with your pâté in a few ticks, sir.'

'Thank you, cook,' he replied. 'Thank you very much indeed.'

He settled down to the soup she'd served, and found the hot rich broth delicious and comforting. As he looked at the empty place across from him, he had to admit he missed having Elizabeth nearby. Damn, but she was a delightful temptress and no mistake.

Meanwhile, at the backdoor Elizabeth had just finished cleaning his boots. There was dirt under her fingernails, but she was too generally bedraggled to care. She placed Smithy's cleaning supplies neatly back in the box, exactly as she had found them, then returned it to the cupboard. It did not occur to her that she was being so diligent because it was the right thing to do, nor did she ponder the thought of further punishment if she left a mess. She was too tired to consider that she never put things away after her, that it had always been someone else's job to run around in her wake.

As she placed Lord Michael's boots against the wall, beneath the hat rack, she actually smiled with pride. They positively shone with lustre, and she congratulated herself on a job very well done.

She could now, finally, go up to her room and soak away her aches in a steaming hot tub.

She trudged to the back stairs and went up them as fast as her weary bones would allow. The pain from the switch had eased, and as soon as she made her way into the bedroom she began peeling off her dishevelled and grubby clothes. By the time she was in her bathroom she was already undressed, and she turned on the taps full force. She lovingly eyed the hot, steaming water, willing it to fill the tub quickly. She threw in some scented oil, and before the bath was even half full she gingerly lowered herself in.

The punished flesh of her bottom protested and she

winced slightly, then sighed as she sunk down, and laying her head back, closed her eyes, listening to the comforting sound of the running water. Never before had a bath felt so good. Poor Smithy, she thought; she had gathered only one load of wood and cleaned only one pair of boots, whereas he spent all day every day doing that and more and a million and one other chores around the house and grounds. How on earth did he do it?

With the tub full she leaned forward and turned off the taps. With the cake of soap she began scrubbing her hands and arms, and then scrubbed her nails. It was quite a job, but she managed to get them clean, then she craned back her neck until her head was submerged, and felt her knotty tresses loosen in the freeing movement of the fragrant water. When satisfied she lifted her head, lounged back, closed her eyes, and relaxed.

Her mind drifted to a bitterly cold winter night, snow on the ground outside, a large soft bed, and he was standing over her. The fire danced in the hearth, casting moving shadows around the room, and he leaned down, kissing her gently on the lips.

'You are a very good girl,' he said tenderly. 'You need a firm hand, but you are a very good girl.'

She moaned with pleasure, a shiver ran through her and her eyes popped open. She didn't know how long she had been there, but now the water was barely warm. She was about to call to Grace when her smarting bottom reminded her that the maid was not available. She also realised she was hungry, so she got out of the tub, dried herself quickly, and wrapped her hair in a towel.

Then she went to her dresser, chose a set of fresh underwear, pulled them on, tying them hurriedly, then opening the door of her wardrobe grabbed the first thing she saw. It was a very simple white cotton frock.

Unwrapping the damp towel she then ran a brush through her hair to clear any tangles. Normally she would have spent an age making sure it was just right, but on this occasion vanity was the last thing on her mind.

Finally she slipped on a pair of satin slippers.

Almost running along the landing and down the back stairs she exploded into the kitchen, startling cook, who was just putting some dishes away.

'Heavens, girl!' she exclaimed. 'You near gave me a heart attack, bursting in here like that.'

'I'm so sorry, cook,' she panted.

Cook almost fell over; in all the years she had worked for the family it was the first time she'd heard the young lady apologise. She would never have spoken to Elizabeth in the manner that she had either, had it not been for Lord Michael's attitude. Like a common girl from the neighbourhood, he had said. Well, if a common girl from the neighbourhood had come rushing in that way she would have spoken to her exactly as she had. And if cook had known her well, a sharp rap across the knuckles with her wooden spoon would not have been far behind. 'Sit yourself down then,' she said, bustling about, removing Elizabeth's lunch from the stove.

Elizabeth had rarely felt so hungry in her life, and everything she ate tasted delicious, and by the end of the simple meal she was showering cook with compliments.

'My, you were hungry, Miss Elizabeth,' said the bustling woman. 'You're usually such a picky eater.'

Elizabeth sat back in her chair and sighed. 'Well, I've had quite a busy morning, cook,' she disclosed.

The ruddy woman suppressed a smile, wondering just what Lord Michael had been up to. 'His lordship is waiting for you in the sitting room,' she announced, delivering his message. 'He wanted to see you after you finished your meal.'

To cook's surprise the young woman jumped up from the scrubbed pine table, thanked her a second time and left the kitchen, obviously eager not to keep the gentleman waiting.

Lord Michael was resting easily in a capacious armchair, the cool afternoon a perfect excuse for a fire. He had allowed himself the luxury of imagining how sweet it would be to feel Elizabeth's lissom body laying submissively beside him, but the sound of the sitting room door opening brought him back to the moment. He looked up.

'My lord,' Elizabeth said, shyly entering the room. She looked quite angelic in her simple white cotton dress.

'Come here, Elizabeth,' he said fondly.

She walked over, instinctively kneeling in front of him as if it was the most natural thing in the world to do. The fire cast her in a warm glow.

Her hair, still quite damp, was falling in haphazard ringlets to her shoulders, and the cotton dress showed off her figure enticingly, outlining her nipples. He felt himself stir, and allowed the comfortable silence to hang in the air as he inhaled the fresh scent of her. He adored how she was kneeling before him, her eyes filled with uneasy expectancy.

He gently guided her cheek to rest upon his knee, closed his eyes and stroked her hair. Her lustrous curls wrapped around his fingers, and he couldn't help but imagine the taking of her maidenhead, feeling himself stir again mere inches from her soft lips.

'Elizabeth,' he said, and she raised her head to look at

him. 'Tell me how you feel.'

She thought for a moment, before saying, 'Full of grace, sir.'

He had asked many women to describe their initial feelings in submission, and had never heard it phrased so eloquently. He reached under her arms and pulled her up onto his lap, and she snuggled into him.

'That's very good to know, Elizabeth,' he whispered.

'I wish only to please you, sir,' she replied softly, surprising herself with the sincerity of the response.

He placed a hand under her chin, raising her face. He touched his lips to hers and she quivered, thrilled by the kiss. His lips travelled to her cheek, kissed her lightly a few times, then slowly down to her throat, just beneath her delicate ear, feeling her gentle pulse. She swooned and felt completely breathless, and gasped as she felt a strong hand cup one of her breasts, sending a dizzying chill down her spine, making her tremble.

Reluctantly he moved his hand from her soft breast, and took a deep breath. 'All right, Elizabeth,' he said, regaining his composure. 'Let me take a good look at you. Stand up.'

She had difficulty obeying the instruction. Her knees were weak and she felt quite faint, to the extent that he steadied her as she rose from his lap, then catching her breath she stood obediently in front of him.

'You're not terribly well turned out, are you, Elizabeth?' he commented, frowning a little.

She felt her face flush. 'No, sir,' she admitted, now sorry she had not taken more time and trouble over her appearance.

'Why is that? Do I not warrant care and attention to your person?'

'Oh, yes sir, of course you do, sir,' she said insistently. 'I was just hungry and therefore in a hurry,' she answered, knowing it was a feeble excuse.

'That is not acceptable, Elizabeth,' he admonished sternly. Go back up to your room and make yourself more presentable. Before you do, however, bring me my boots for inspection. I trust they are well polished?'

'Yes sir,' she replied. 'You'll have no cause for complaint, sir.'

'Off you go then, and be quick about it.' With an indifferent wave he dismissed Elizabeth as though suddenly intensely bored of her presence, and she could not quite believe how deep that attitude stung her – only a few hours before she would not have cared one jot about what he, or anyone for that matter, thought of her.

As the door closed behind her Lord Michael inhaled deeply. He stood up and paced back and forth in front of the fire, deep in thought. He simply did not normally respond to women in such a profound way as this. He wandered over to the windows and gazed distractedly out. The beauty of the grounds calmed him, but something on the floor, near the desk, caught his eye.

Looking down he spied Elizabeth's fine underwear. He had completely forgotten all about it. Recalling the immense pleasure of sliding the sensuous material across her shapely bottom, he reached down and picked up the delicate lingerie. Then raising it to his face he breathed in her fragrance, feeling his member stir yet again. Tonight, he decided, deeply inhaling her body's essence. Tonight, she would be his.

He put the underwear in his pocket, and by the time the luscious girl returned, carrying his heavy boots, he had regained his equanimity.

'Bring them here,' he ordered. 'I shall inspect them whilst you make yourself presentable,' he said, his voice firm.

'Yes, sir,' she replied, strangely happy to obey, and moved towards him.

His eyes fell to her breasts, easily admired within the cotton dress. It would be delightful indeed, he pondered, to suck and kiss those orbs of youthful perfection.

Elizabeth placed the boots on the floor in front of him and even dropped a curtsy, and the charming show of good manners interrupted his erotic thoughts. 'Good girl,' he said.

'Thank you, sir,' she said, bobbing again, 'I'll change and be back in just a few minutes.'

'Wait,' he said, stopping her. 'You'd better take these with you.' Reaching into his pocket he withdrew the panties and handed them to her. Blushing, she took the intimate apparel from his hands, then turned and left the room.

Gathering his thoughts he picked up his boots and looked them over carefully. There was not a speck of grime to be found, and they shone as though new. She had done an excellent job on them, but he was not surprised. Despite her questionable attitude she was bright and talented, and now he had started to work on the former he would have expected no less from her. He would have to remain firm with her, however, and stay on his masterly toes.

The mid-afternoon sun was streaming into the room through the large windows, and by the time she returned he had made up his mind; they were going for another walk. When she entered the room he could not suppress a contented smile.

59

Her hair was pinned up, with a few loose curls delicately framing her lovely face. She was attired in a pale blue dress of the finest silk, with a small and charming bow at her throat. It fitted her perfectly, accentuating her mouth-watering breasts, her alluringly narrow waist, and her voluptuous hips. Her dainty feet were encased in cream lace-up boots.

'That's much better, Elizabeth,' he complimented her. 'Much, much better.'

'Thank you, sir,' she said, blushing coyly.

'And now I should like to take some air and enjoy a leisurely stroll with a well-dressed and well-mannered young lady. Do you know anyone who fits that description?'

She looked down coyly, uncertain of the game he was playing. 'I believe, sir... that I might be able to satisfy,' she ventured, hoping it was the right thing to say. 'If it pleases you, sir.'

He nodded thoughtfully. 'Excellent,' he said, offering his elbow. 'I very much think you might, at that. Take my arm and we shall proceed together.'

Leaving the shining boots beside the fire and his vacated chair, her arm looped through his, they left the sitting room.

Chapter Seven

The walk through the gardens was pleasant indeed. They shared conversation and comfortable silences, and both felt utterly at ease in the other's company, staying to the paths and avoiding the wet lawns.

There was a crispness in the air that was pleasing to them both, and as they made their way around the landscaped grounds he could not help but think what delightful company she had become, and so quickly. The autumn fragrances from the manicured borders, mixed with the exotic perfume uniquely hers, were all rather heady.

And Elizabeth was elated. Despite the difference in their years she had finally met someone who warranted her respect and adoration. Just a few hours before the last thing on her mind, lying over his knee, her bottom stinging from the smacks of his hand, was that she would be walking with him in such a way, feeling as she did.

Indeed, in those first few minutes she truly hated him; she had seen him as nothing but a bully and a brute. But now she felt she was beginning to understand him. He had been correct in his assessment of her and what she truly deserved and needed.

By the time he guided her back to the house her cheeks were rosy, not just from the fresh air and exercise, but also from the naughty stirrings in her body. And as for Lord Michael, he was quite beside himself with desire for her.

Dusk had descended and he suggested they both take a rest before dinner. As he walked her into the house he took her elbow and they ascended the stairs together, and he continued to hold it as they made their way along the landing to her room.

She opened the door, smiling, but to her instant dismay she realised she had carelessly left her previous clothes strewn untidily about. The simple cotton dress, from which she had changed so quickly, lay on the floor, and a trail of grimy clothes, remnants from the morning's events, led from the middle of the room to the bathroom.

'Oh dear,' he said, eyeing and assessing the mess instantly, his manner suddenly brusque, 'what do we have here, Elizabeth?'

Her heart jumped. 'I, um, I d-don't seem to have put my things away.' The obvious was all she could feebly stammer.

'No, you certainly have not,' he said, his tone leaving no doubt about his displeasure. 'And I consider it a personal insult that you should allow me to see your room in such a poor state of tidiness. Fetch me your hairbrush, Elizabeth.'

She looked up at him, instantly understanding his intention, beseeching him silently, but he was unmoved. So she walked to her dresser, knowing all the while that he was right to be displeased with her. She should never have left things as she had, expecting them to be miraculously picked up and dispensed with without consideration.

'What a mess,' he said, closing the bedroom door. 'You really are very slovenly, Elizabeth. It's just as well I came up to see this, isn't it?' He looked around. It was a fashionable room indeed; artfully and stylishly decorated, all the accoutrements a young lady could ask for, including a handsome four-poster bed, draped with a flowing, diaphanous white fabric.

There was a full-length mirror, which had two smaller mirrors hinged on either side. A cream-coloured dressing table was placed in the window, allowing her to view the gardens as she groomed herself. Delicate flowers were etched in the wood, painted in pastel shades. He walked to it, and taking the hairbrush from her hand, told her to turn and face the window.

'From now on, Elizabeth,' he said, 'every time you look out this window, you will remember this moment. It might help to remind you that laziness and slovenliness are not permitted or tolerated.'

'Yes, sir,' she replied meekly, head bowed in shame.

During their recent time together Elizabeth had felt a bond growing between her and Lord Michael. She had convinced herself that the punishments that had gone before, though necessary, were history, not to be repeated. But now she realised such was not the case. She was, and suspected she always would be, vulnerable to his disapproval and subject to his discipline.

'Tell me how sloppy you've been,' he told her, 'and ask me for your deserved punishment, Elizabeth.'

She felt the familiar blush rise in her cheeks. 'I... I was very neglectful, sir, in my habits,' she acknowledged quietly. 'And I... I would be grateful if you would see fit to punish me accordingly... sir.'

'Very well,' he nodded. 'You will lift your skirt, drop your knickers, and bend over.'

She felt the tears in her eyes but obediently bent at the waist and leant on the dressing table, her bottom bared for the reprisal her poor show warranted.

He moved behind her and placed himself as he had in the sitting room that very morning, facing into the room with an arm over and around her waist. He ran the smoothly varnished wood of the hairbrush over her naked globes, savouring the evidence of the morning's beatings. Then speaking softly but firmly he lectured her.

'Elizabeth, today you have done well in some respects, but you failed to follow those pluses through. Was it not obvious to you that you should have tidied your own mess? I certainly hope you did not leave it for Grace, for if you did I shall ask *her* to spank you when she returns from her day off.'

'Oh, no sir!' she cried. 'That was not my intention, I assure you!'

'Granted, it is her employment,' he went on, 'but as she's not here the responsibility falls to you, does it not?'

Elizabeth could feel the unforgiving surface of the wood against her flesh, and she prayed – though she did not ask for mercy. 'Yes sir,' she replied despondently.

'And even if Grace were here, it would be easy for you to drop your dirty clothes in the hamper, then lay your clean clothes on the bed. Is that not just good sense and good standards?'

'Yes, sir,' she admitted, knowing he was right and thinking about all the times she had carelessly tossed her clothes on the floor without a second thought.

'A few good smacks and I think you'll remember next time.' He lifted the brush, and it landed with a loud splat on her poor left buttock. She rocked a little in his hold and yelped, and he repeated the action, again and again until he had delivered six stinging blows on each cheek.

'What do you say now?' he asked, panting very slightly from the immensely enjoyable exertion.

'Thank you, sir,' she sniffled. 'I'm very sorry, sir, it won't happen again.'

'See that it doesn't,' he said sharply, with little apparent warmth towards her. 'Now take your nap and I'll see you at dinner.'

With that he placed the brush back on Elizabeth's dresser and strode from the room, leaving her head spinning in utter confusion as to his intentions toward her, and her bottom throbbing warmly.

After dinner Lord Michael eyed his polished boots as he sat comfortably in front of the fire, the delicious evening meal digesting, a glass of brandy in one hand, Elizabeth quietly sitting opposite him, the crackling fire making her face glow healthily.

'I must say, you did an excellent job on those, Elizabeth,' he said, nodding at his shining footwear.

'Thank you, sir,' she replied. 'I've never cleaned boots before, so I wasn't quite sure what I was doing or how well I'd done.'

'I'll just take them up to my room,' he went on. 'You wait here. I'll only be a moment.'

Leaving her by the fire he made his way upstairs, and as he placed his boots beside the dresser he eyed his very best riding crop lying on its top.

Downstairs Elizabeth was already becoming a little bored in her own company. Patience had never been her strong suit, and to her he seemed to be taking a long time. She decided to get another bottle of champagne, and to prove to him she had learned a thing or two, she would find the wine stock herself.

She went to the kitchen, but to her dismay cook told her she was too busy for such things and she would have to go down to the cellars for the champagne. So, with the best of intentions, Elizabeth made her way along the gloomy passage at the back of the house, normally only used by the servants, and as she passed the footman's quarters she thought she heard a strange noise. Yes, there it was again; a rhythmic creaking, almost ghostly sound, and as she listened more intently she was sure she could hear some sort of moaning too!

Surely no servants were in the house, apart from cook, she puzzled. What could the sounds possibly be?

With inquisitiveness getting the better of her, and breathlessly keen to discover more, she very quietly pushed down on the door handle, carefully eased it open an inch or two… and could not believe her eyes! There, bathed in dim lamplight was Grace, naked, on her hands and knees! And Billy, the old gardener's young help, was kneeling behind her, his face strangely contorted as he thrust his hips at the servant girl with astonishing ferocity that made her breasts quiver and swing back and forth.

Elizabeth stood rooted to the spot for a moment, utterly stunned by the scene. She knew she should close the door, leave the couple to their privacy, and go straight to the cellar for the champagne, but she was utterly transfixed. Completely mesmerised. She could not take her eyes off them, and so engrossed were they in their lovemaking they had no idea she was there.

Meanwhile Lord Michael, returning to the sitting room, was puzzled to find it empty. Seeing the empty champagne bottle on the occasional table he astutely suspected that his young supplicant had gone looking for more to drink, so he decided to visit the kitchen to find her, and found cook still clearing the dinner things up. In response to his query she confirmed that Elizabeth had indeed gone down to the cellars to collect a fresh bottle for them. So as he found and made his way along the dingy passageway he stopped in his tracks, for Elizabeth was there, just ahead of him in the shadows, peering through a surreptitiously ajar door. He frowned; what on earth was she doing?

Silently he approached, and standing behind her, looking over her shoulder, he was able to see the young couple making love, completely unaware of two pairs of prying eyes, and the fact that she was sneakily invading their privacy smacked as an instant affront to his integrity.

Without hesitation he grabbed her around the waist, clamped a hand over her mouth so she couldn't cry out, and with his other hand, though still holding his favourite riding crop, he managed to quickly but silently close the door. He then bustled her back along the passageway as covertly as he could, whispering fiercely into her ear that she was not to make a sound, and as soon as they were out of earshot of the kitchen he let her go, pushing her in front of him, and brought the crop down upon her bottom with a severity that shocked her more than hurt her. Her dress and petticoat shielded most of the blow, but when she turned to face him the anger on his face made her positively tremble.

'You despicable sneak!' he scolded her. 'Have you learned nothing today? Spying on your unsuspecting servants while they steal a moment or two together? What shameful behaviour!'

'Oh, sir, please don't be angry with me!' she wailed, truly upset that she had failed him, and fearful of the consequences. 'I'm sorry!' she cried.

'You have disappointed me, Elizabeth,' he said, catching his breath. 'Go up to your room at once. You must be severely punished for this. You are a very, very naughty young lady.'

She burst into tears and ran upstairs, holding up her skirt so as not to trip. She threw open her bedroom door and landed facedown on her bed, scolding herself for her stupidity. All her plans to please him were gone. Just like that, out of the window.

Soon she heard him as he made his way along the landing, his footfalls sounding heavy and determined, as though he had a serious duty to perform and perform it he would, no matter what.

Lord Michael approached her open door, rapping the crop against his leg with each stride and making sure she could hear its potent threat; anxious anticipation always increased the effectiveness of a good chastisement in the recipient.

When he entered her room he almost felt sorry for her, but didn't show it. Her splendid dress was rumpled underneath her, her hair was slightly askew, and as she turned and looked up at him with imploring eyes her flushed cheeks glistened with tears.

'Oh, my lord, please, please forgive me,' she pleaded, almost melting his resolve.

But he reached back and closed the door without taking his eyes from her, and then approached the bed upon which she sprawled. 'I'm sorry, young lady, but you need to be disciplined for such underhand behaviour. Someone of your high breeding and station should not stoop to such levels. You will learn that nothing you do, good or bad, is without consequence. You have disappointed me, for I thought you already understood that.'

'Oh, I do, sir,' she sobbed, 'believe me I do.'

'Then you must realise that your behaviour was wrong, and you must pay the price.'

'Yes, sir,' she said, dropping her head.

'Take off your dress and underwear; I want you only in your petticoat,' he ordered. 'And when you've done that, fetch me some of your scarves.'

'Yes, sir,' she said, calming a little but puzzled by the latter demand.

As she undressed, from the corner of her eye she noticed him take off his jacket and cravat, remove his cufflinks and roll up his sleeves, which unsettled her again. But in her petticoat and bare feet she found the scarves he wanted and stood, full of trepidation, awaiting further instructions.

'Stand at the foot of the bed, Elizabeth, and grip the nearest post,' he instructed, and trembling slightly she did as she was told. 'I am going to bind your wrists, young lady, and as I punish you, you will take care not to scream, for if you do a gag is not far behind.'

'Yes, s-sir,' she stammered.

He was efficient in his work, and when finished tying her wrists to the ornately carved post he lifted her petticoat, exposing her bottom to his appreciation. Then plucking up another scarf he wrapped it around her waist, holding her petticoat up and out of the way. She was now naked from the waist down, and shivered with embarrassment and fear.

Picking up the crop, he then addressed her again. 'Elizabeth, you will now receive three extremely significant strokes from my crop. Do you understand?'

'Yes, sir,' she answered breathlessly.

'Are you ready?' he asked, his voice without apparent emotion.

'Yes, sir,' she replied, cringing.

He placed the crop across the upper slope of her bottom,

leaving it there a moment. Then he lifted it and waited. He heard Elizabeth let out a soft moan, and then he swept it down, the leather implement emitting a pleasing *crack!* as it found its mark.

Elizabeth gasped and clenched her teeth, but did not cry out.

He placed the crop against her once again, an inch or so below the bright red line of the first stroke. He raised it, and bringing it down with another practiced sweep of his arm it landed accurately, exploding in a second raised stripe.

Again she took it stoically and did not scream.

Lord Michael repeated his actions for the third time, and when the crop cut into the fleshy lower part of her bottom Elizabeth hissed, threw her head back, clutched the bedpost even tighter, and stamped her foot once on the floor.

He held the crop to her parted lips. 'Kiss it, Elizabeth,' he whispered. 'Kiss that which teaches you right from wrong.'

Large tears were squeezing from her eyes as she kissed the cruel crop. Her bottom was on fire, but her tears were more from shame and humiliation than from the punishment itself. He stood beside her, gently caressing her tortured flesh. 'Your training must now continue,' he told her, 'and it will not all be just about discipline.'

'It… it won't?' she whimpered, loving the feel of his hand on her burning bottom.

'No, it won't,' he said, untying her wrists. 'First, I am going to move you.' Holding her by the waist he walked her over to the window. The curtain rod was solid oak, strong and well secured. He lifted her arms, tying them to it above her head.

'Are you sorry, Elizabeth?' he asked, dropping his hands

to caress her bottom cheeks again.

'I am very sorry, sir,' she sniffled, comforted by his soothing hands.

'Good…' he quietly comforted, 'now part your legs and close your eyes…'

He stood quietly next to her for a moment, making sure she was secure and comfortable, and then began to stroke the insides of her thighs. She gasped with surprise, and then sighed pleasurably.

'How does that feel, Elizabeth?' he asked.

'Wonderful, sir,' she replied honestly.

'I'm going to touch you somewhere else now, my dear,' he said, preparing her. 'Do you know where I mean?'

'Um, yes sir,' she whispered carefully, filled with tantalising apprehension. 'I think I do, sir.'

He trailed his fingers up her thighs, and then brushed her pussy lips, barely touching her clit. She gasped and wriggled slightly. He ventured further. His fingers found her wet and open. She arched her back, pushing against his hand. He slipped a finger between her swollen lips, and she moaned.

He pulled his hand away and slipped his arm around her waist, gently kissing the back of her neck, pressing himself against her. His hand moved up to her breast, pinched her nipple under the smooth silk, then began to caress and knead the soft orb. His breath was on her shoulders, and he felt her nipple grow hard under his touch. She was trembling, and he knew it was from a deep, carnal lust.

He broke away and Elizabeth groaned in disappointment. She wanted him next to her, touching her most secret places. She could hear him move around the room and silently prayed he would quickly return, and continue to do those deliciously unspeakable things to her. She could feel her wanton wetness, she could feel her lips parted in need, and she ached for his hands on her body.

Lord Michael dowsed all the lamps except one. It cast a warm glow around the room, and she breathed a wanting whimper as she heard him approach again. 'How are you feeling?' he whispered, his breath hot in her ear.

'I, um, I don't feel quite normal,' she stuttered, not sure how to explain the hot urges racing through her body, or the scandalous desires dancing in her mind.

'I am going to give you a choice, Elizabeth,' he said, 'which is not something I do very often. So I want you to listen very carefully.'

A choice? Elizabeth stiffened. A choice of what?

'I can untie you, put you to your bed, and the evening will be over,' he explained. 'You will never have to be dealt with by me again. Never be spanked or whipped, never have to perform menial tasks because I say so, never be made to do things you don't want to do. It will be as though today and this evening never happened.'

Elizabeth felt a panic rising from the pit of her tummy. He was going to leave her? She could hardly bear the thought.

'Or, you can ask me to stay,' he continued. 'You can ask me to carry on with your training – for that is what I have been doing today – to teach you about your mind and body and spirit, and all they have to offer. The choice is yours, Elizabeth. Do I stay with you tonight, or do I leave you now?'

So those were her choices, and she did not hesitate to follow her heart.

'Oh sir, please stay,' she begged. 'Please stay with me!'

Lord Michael's lips brushed her shoulder and neck, and she moaned, feeling the pleasure pulsate through her. 'Very well, Elizabeth, I shall stay,' he murmured.

'Oh, thank you, sir,' she cried with gratitude and relief as he pressed against her, and she realised he was now naked. His hands were around her, cupping her breasts, his tongue tracing the contours of her dainty ear. She moaned, surrendering to his contact, desperately wanting him to touch her down there again, but too embarrassed to ask.

But as if reading her thoughts he asked, 'What would you like me to do now, Elizabeth?'

'Whatever… whatever pleases you, sir.'

'It's all right, Elizabeth,' he reassured her, 'on this occasion you can tell me what would please you.'

'Please, sir, would you touch me…' she whispered, feeling flustered and embarrassed to be thinking what she was thinking, never mind saying it to a man – an older man who was still little more than a stranger, 'would you touch me lower… between my legs, sir?'

Lord Michael smiled, his hardness pressing against her naked bottom, and he moved his hands down her front. His fingers burrowed between her thighs, teasing her, and she held her breath in anticipation.

'Oh, *God*,' she heard herself gasp. 'More… please, more.'

He moved his fingers and slowly manipulated her clitoris. She cried out, her legs all but giving way, but the bonds were secure and as he continued to play with her, dancing his fingers across her swollen bud, she felt something strange building within her.

Her breathing became panting, and sobs crept from her throat. He increased his movements, making them more assertive. She pressed back against him, responding even more passionately, and he knew her release was near. He stopped then and she moaned desperately. He was powerfully erect and needing to fuck her.

'You are a saucy little minx, aren't you?' he goaded.

She didn't respond, but her breathing was deep and her breasts were rising and falling with unquenched passion. He reached up and untied her, and as her wrists fell he swooped her up in his arms.

He laid her on the bed, pulled her petticoat up and over her head leaving her completely naked, then stretched alongside her, staring at her beauty. Her breasts were full and ripe. They felt soft but firm as he began caressing them again. Hungrily he laid his lips on her nipples, sucking and biting.

Lying over the supine beauty he laced his fingers in her hair, pressing his lips to hers, and slipped his tongue into her mouth. She wrapped her arms around his neck, pulling him closer. They kissed deeply, tongues dancing, and then he began to move down her body.

'Be very still,' he said, commanding her quietly.

She almost held her breath but it was impossible, and as he moved further and further down she could feel herself still trembling. His fingers separated her sex lips, something amazing and delicious flicked her clit, and she felt them inside her. 'Oh sir, please?' she begged. 'There's a need in me I cannot begin to describe.'

Suddenly she was rolled over. He grabbed her hips, pulled her up to her knees, and then spanked her with his open palm. She squealed as the unexpected slaps assailed her bottom.

'You will have that special moment when I say, Elizabeth,' he said firmly, 'and not before.' Then softening his voice, he continued. 'You have surrendered your body. I shall do with it as I please. Learn to enjoy it, my dear,

74

for it will be your greatest pleasure.'

He admired and caressed her punished cheeks, then slipped his fingers between her pussy lips again, touching her sensitive, swollen clit. 'Do you understand?' he pressed.

'Yes, sir,' she whispered repentantly, moving against his teasing hand.

'Good. Then just relax and feel, and soon you will know what it means to surrender to pleasure. To become a sweet, submissive girl.'

She let out a long deep sigh as he kept her on her hands and knees, his fingers and lips and tongue exploring her. He continued his salacious play until she was desperate, all reasoned thought having abandoned her, and then he placed his cock against her wet entrance.

'Do you want me, my dear?' he asked.

'Yes, sir,' she panted, succumbing to the hedonistic craving. 'I think I do.'

'How much?' he asked, pushing a little with his hips.

'Oh, sir, if it pleases, I think I want you very much…'

His fingers moved under her, touching her tender bud, and once again he started to fondle her. She gasped in pleasure, her head dropping between her arms, but his free hand grabbed her hair, pulling it back as he pressed into her, slowly but insistently.

Carefully, pressing in a little further, he suddenly felt it – her body's natural resistance. She felt it too and let out a little cry of uncertainty.

'Are you ready, my sweet Elizabeth?' he asked. 'I warn you, it will hurt a little.'

'Oh yes, sir, *please* sir,' she begged.

Lord Michael moved his hands back and held her hips, pulled back, and then with a strong thrust he penetrated the kneeling girl with one inexorable movement. She uttered a cry and he pulled back, repeated the action, and this time he felt her give and tightly accommodate his full length and girth.

'Almost there, my dear,' he grunted. 'A moment's more discomfort and then naught but pleasure.'

'Yes sir, I'm fine sir,' she whimpered bravely, not at all sure it was true as the man withdrew again, then sank forward and buried himself deeply and fully inside her. 'Oh!' she cried, clenching her fists and clutching the bedcover.

He rested inside her for a minute, letting her feel him, then slowly began to fuck her. Smoothly and easily he slid in and out of her delicious and vulnerable body. She was tight and tense, so he moved his fingers beneath her again, touching her clit, and she immediately began to relax, her state of arousal renewed. Moments later she began to press back against him, meeting his movements with her own.

He gradually increased the tempo, thrusting in and out with vigour, his fingers working artfully between her pussy lips. She began to groan, louder and louder, until he knew her moment was nigh. As was his.

'If you feel your moment, Elizabeth, embrace it,' he ordered.

She was completely silent for a moment, holding her breath, waiting, not even sure what she was waiting for. A new feeling had grown inside her. His fingers were rubbing aggressively, his cock pumping, and then suddenly an explosion rocked her. As the spasms took hold she sank her face into the pillows to muffle the screams of sheer bliss that erupted from deep in her lungs.

Her inner walls gripped him tightly and her body

shuddered as she climaxed, the orgasm surging through her. It was enough to send him over the edge too, and he pumped strongly, feeling his own explosive release.

Eventually, their passions spent, their ragged movements eased and their rasping breathing calmed. Lord Michael released her hips, his softening penis slipping from her, and she collapsed on the bed. Stretching out he rolled her with him so they were side by side, and tenderly swept the damp tendrils of hair from her hot cheek. He stroked her breasts, and waited for her breathing to calm. Again she sighed deeply.

'How do you feel, my dear?' he asked.

She didn't respond right away, but then just when he was about to ask again she said, 'It's so hard to describe, sir. I feel tranquil, yet invigorated.'

'You know you've turned a corner in your young life, don't you? You've taken the first few steps on a long but wonderful journey.'

'Yes, sir,' she replied, too happy and overcome to truly understand the depth of his words. 'I think I know that.'

'Rest now. You've had a very long day.'

'Mmm, and night,' she murmured, feeling her eyes close and sleep float about her.

Lord Michael cradled the shapely young beauty, finding it difficult to accept the unfamiliar feelings he too was experiencing.

Chapter Eight

Lord Michael stayed with Elizabeth throughout the night. She would stir in her sleep and feel him snuggled against her, or his arm thrown over her. She had never felt so safe, nor so at peace. Though she slept lightly, not used to sharing her bed, she loved having his warm, strong body next to her.

In the early hours of the morning he cuddled her close, whispered in her ear that he must leave her, and retreated to his room. She wanted him to stay but already knew better than to ask, and once alone between the sheets she held his pillow close, smelt the masculine memory of him on the linen, and drifted back off to sleep.

And when Grace entered and opened the curtains the girl barely moved.

'Morning, Miss Elizabeth,' the maid said in her usual manner. 'It's a bit later than usual, but Lord Michael said to let you rest this morning. It's almost ten o'clock.'

Elizabeth could not believe it was so late. She rarely slept past eight, and certainly Grace never woke her later than eight-thirty. Even so she felt tired, and smiled to herself; it was not surprising after all she'd been through. She heard Grace running a bath, and stretching languidly, raised herself onto her elbows, squinting in the morning light bathing her bed.

'I'll have cook fix you a late breakfast, Miss Elizabeth,' Grace said, closing the bathroom door so as to keep in the warmth. 'Will there be anything else?'

'No, thank you, Grace,' the sleepy girl said, suppressing a yawn and suddenly blushing as the scene she'd witnessed in the servants area of her father's house the night before flooded back to her. The image of Grace kneeling and jerking back and forth as young Billy fucked her like one of the rams out in the fields, and suddenly she viewed the maid in a different light, with a degree of respectful admiration. 'No, that will be all.'

The maid curtsied, clearly surprised that her mistress was being so agreeable. Usually first thing in the morning Miss Elizabeth wasn't the nicest person to be around.

Elizabeth flopped the bedcovers back and padded her way to the bathroom, feeling a little jaded and the threat of a possible headache looming. A late night and too much champagne, she thought wistfully, and slothfully began her morning ablutions.

By the time she made it downstairs it felt closer to lunch than breakfast. But eggs and toast and a cup of tea sounded exactly right, so she sat down at the dining table and was very pleased when she discovered that was exactly what awaited her.

She wondered where the wonderful Lord Michael was, so finishing her meal she wandered the house in search of him, ending up in the sitting room overlooking the gardens. She sighed a happy sigh; how much she adored him and how quickly those feelings had blossomed. It was there, in this very room, that he had first turned her over his knee. She could not believe it was less than twenty-four hours earlier. But how she had thought him such a brute then, and oh, how he instead turned out to be the man of her dreams, despite his mature age compared to her tender years.

As she pondered him and the wondrous night they had

79

spent together she coughed unexpectedly, and sniffled a little.

'There you are, Elizabeth.' It was him! 'Are you feeling all right?'

Glowing with happiness she turned to face him. 'Good morning, sir, I hope you slept well,' she said daringly.

He raised an eyebrow, gave her a severe look, and then relaxed and laughed. 'Yes, thank you, I slept very well indeed. And you?'

'Oh, very well, thank you. Never better.' She coughed again and Lord Michael frowned.

'Are you sure you're all right?' he asked again, genuine concern in his voice.

'Yes,' she insisted, 'it's just a bit of a tickle in my throat, nothing more.'

'Hmmm, well you look a little peaky to me,' he adjudged. 'Come here.'

Dutifully she walked over to him, and he touched his palm to her forehead. 'Elizabeth, you are very warm,' he decided, 'and your eyes, they're a little dull. I think you're coming down with something.'

'No, I'm fine, sir, really.' If he thought she was off colour he might make her spend the day alone in bed, and she certainly did not want that.

'Well, if you say so,' he said, unconvinced. 'Now, I've some work I must see to. It is going to take me an hour or so, so you amuse yourself until I'm finished, and then after lunch we'll spend the afternoon together.'

A fresh cough threatened to burst forth, and she did her best to suppress it. 'I think I'll take Constance out for some exercise,' she managed. Constance was her beautiful bay mare, and if Lord Michael was going to leave her to her own devices for an hour or so, there was nothing she

80

would rather do than take her horse for a stirring gallop.

Lord Michael looked at her quizzically, his brow furrowing. 'Elizabeth, I do not think that's such a good idea.' He walked briskly over to the windows. 'It's a little blustery outside, and there's some weather threatening. You'd best stay indoors and keep warm by the fire.'

'But sir—'

'You would not be attempting to question me, would you, Elizabeth?'

She felt the colour rise in her cheeks, studied the floor for a moment, and then replied demurely that she was not.

'As far as I'm concerned you are not quite well, despite what you say,' he continued, 'and it will not do you any good to be out in the brisk air. Besides, I believe rain is threatening, so you will stay in here by the fire.'

Elizabeth sighed with resignation. 'Yes, sir.'

'Now, I have my work to be getting on with,' he went on, the issue decided in accordance with his ruling, naturally, although he recognised with satisfaction that a day earlier would have seen a more confrontational stance from the girl. 'I will be in your father's study, and I do not want to be disturbed under any circumstances. Do you understand?' She nodded demurely, and feeling pleased with the progress being made, he turned and left the room.

Elizabeth was bored again. It seemed she'd been left alone an eternity. Meandering back to the window she stared up at the sky, feeling decidedly cooped up, although the sun was peeking out from behind admittedly dark clouds.

Even more bored and sulky than she had been five minutes before, she went up to her room. The sun was shining in, and though she could see the blustery wind blowing the trees around, it seemed to be an invigorating day and too good to be virtually imprisoned.

'Oh bother!' she exclaimed; despite the occasional tickle in her throat she felt perfectly all right, the previously threatening headache never having arrived. Lord Michael had forbidden her to go outside because he thought her unwell, but she was feeling fine. Yes, definitely fine. But since he had left specific instructions that he was not to be disturbed, she could not exactly inform him of that. No, there was no doubt in her mind that she was perfectly all right and there was no reason why she should not go for a ride.

Her mind made up, she hastily donned her riding clothes, raced down the stairs two at a time, and out to the stables.

Lord Michael sat back and stretched his arms, his neck a little stiff. He laid down the pen and stood up. The latest business venture was requiring a greater investment in time than he had anticipated, and the figures were difficult to make sense of. He wandered over to the window, gazing out, not really seeing anything, mulling over the options available to him, when suddenly the shock of seeing Elizabeth cantering across the fields on her mare, the spirited horse tossing its head, was not to be believed!

'Good lord!' he exclaimed. 'Will she never learn that I mean what I say?'

He was immediately angry; yet again she was being grossly disobedient. How dare she? Yet watching her despite his ire he had to admit she was a spellbinding sight. Even in his anger he had to admire the wonderful vision – beauty and power in perfect harmony.

The mare left the ground and jumped effortlessly over

a fallen tree trunk, Elizabeth staying with her, making it look easy. They galloped out of view and he craned his neck to follow, but they were gone.

Pulling out his pocket watch he checked the time. It was eleven-fifty. Well, there was little he could do, so he'd go back to work and see what the young culprit had to say for herself when they met for lunch. He was determined she would pay severely for her flagrant disobedience.

He settled back at the desk, and had just begun to make some more notes when there was a rumbling boom and a jagged flash of lightening across the increasingly angry sky outside. Large droplets of rain splattered against the windowpanes, and they were quickly growing in intensity. His anger quickly turned to concern. She was going to get caught in a downpour, and her fledgling cold could turn into something very much more serious. Not to mention the distinct possibility that her horse might spook in the storm and throw her. So he hurried out of the study, through the large house, and grabbed a raincoat as he dashed out of the backdoor, racing to the stables.

Elizabeth was indeed caught in the deluge and Constance was not happy at all, but Elizabeth was able to handle her. She managed to get the mare turned around and they galloped back towards the house. She was getting soaked through, and the cold rain had her teeth chattering.

Lord Michael was just about to mount a horse and go out to search for her when he heard clattering hooves on the cobblestones outside the stable. He ran to the open stable door and saw the large bay mare being reined in by a totally drenched and bedraggled Elizabeth. Leaving his horse to the stable boy he dashed out into the rain to help her. She saw him, dragged her feet out of the stirrups and slumped gratefully to the ground, leaning against his body for support. She was shaking so badly from the cold and wet he could barely hold her up while Constance, now free of her rider, trotted into the shelter of the stable.

'Elizabeth, you are such a silly girl,' he scolded her, although filled with concern. 'Come on, let's get you indoors quickly.'

Her teeth chattered and she couldn't speak from the chill, and felt faint and weak. Her skin turned a horrible grey hue and he recognised the symptoms immediately, so he swept her up and carried her through the driving rain, across the small lawn in the herb garden and in through the backdoor of the house.

'Grace!' he called loudly the minute they were inside. 'Grace!'

The maid wasn't far away at all, polishing some silver in the hall, and hearing the alarm in Lord Michael's voice she dashed to the kitchens, and was shocked by what she saw. Miss Elizabeth, as white as a ghost and drenched to the skin, shivering uncontrollably, being carried by a very wet and very concerned Lord Michael.

'Grace, thank heaven,' he said. 'Run up to Miss Elizabeth's room and draw a hot bath immediately, and pull out some warm bedclothes.'

Without a second glance she dashed out and up the stairs to do as he said. Poor Miss Elizabeth.

'We'll be lucky if you don't catch pneumonia,' he said to the ailing girl cradled in his arms, genuinely afraid that such a thing could happen.

Wrapped up in his arms and out of the driving rain she started to feel a little better, but she was afraid to look at him; and too ashamed, as well, because once again her obstinate nature had gotten her into a dreadful mess.

'We must get you out of these wet things immediately,' he continued, and as quickly as he could he followed the maid and carried Elizabeth up the stairs. When they entered her bedroom he was relieved to find it warm and cosy, a comforting fire already burning nicely in the grate. Grace was running the bath, and there was a thick flannel nightgown laid out upon the bed.

'Thank you, Grace,' he acknowledged the efforts of the maid. 'Now go downstairs and brew some tea. Bring it up nice and hot and sweet.'

'Yes, sir,' the maid said, bobbing politely before she disappeared again.

Elizabeth's shivering was now intermittent, and as soon as Grace had left he carried her to the bathroom, where he stood her on her feet, stripped her quickly, and carefully helped her into the steaming tub.

It felt extremely hot to the chilled Elizabeth and she winced and complained, but the scald only lasted a few seconds, and then the warmth seeped through her flesh into her bones, and her teeth at last stopped their chattering.

Her nose was beginning to run, and Lord Michael, having removed the soaked raincoat, finding his own clothes wet but tolerable, dipped into his pocket and handed her his handkerchief.

'Th-thank you, s-sir,' she said shakily, still too embarrassed to look him in the eye.

'Better get your head under the hot water,' he instructed, and she immediately dipped her head back, the hot water around her head seeming to draw the last of the chill from her.

A moment later, lifting her head, she opened her eyes and finally blinked an apologetic peek up at him through the rivulets of water running down her face. His expression was stern, but his eyes were filled with genuine worry.

'At least you've got some colour back in your cheeks,' he said. 'All right, get out of the tub now. I'll dry you off quickly, then into bed with you right away.'

She stood up without any complaint or any futile attempt to justify her irresponsible behaviour. Lord Michael gave her a towel for her hair, and as she wrapped it around her head he rubbed her with another. As soon as she was dry he hurried her back into the bedroom, and helped her into her long warm nightgown.

'Better dry your hair thoroughly by the fire,' he told her. 'We don't want it to be damp in bed.'

Feeling a lot better and comfortably warmed through to the core again, she gracefully dropped to her knees by the hearth and began to towel her head vigorously, interrupting herself with a few sharp coughs and a sizable sneeze. Lord Michael at last took a deep breath and sat in the chair by her side, removing his wet shoes and socks, when there was a light knock at the door.

It was Grace, and the tray she was carrying contained not just a pot of tea and cups for them both, but bread and honey and some cakes.

'I thought Miss Elizabeth might like a little something to eat,' she said shyly.

'Excellent,' Lord Michael said, smiling appreciatively, 'thank you, Grace, thank you for your help.'

'Can I get anything else for you, sir?' the girl volunteered, blushing beneath his evident appreciation.

'There's a very wet raincoat in the bathroom,' he said. 'Please remove it.'

'Yes, sir.' She hurried into the bathroom and picked up the dripping coat, and wrapped it in a towel to carry it out. 'Can I do anything else for you, sir?' she asked, as she walked back into the bedroom.

'No, thank you, that will be all.'

'Thank you, sir,' she bobbed endearingly again. 'If you need me, I'll be in the kitchen.'

She left, and Lord Michael gazed down at the disobedient young lady kneeling before him. Reaching forward he pulled the soggy towel from her hands. Her head was bowed, and the fire's light flickered off her red highlights. He touched her hair. It was still slightly damp, but no longer wet.

'Elizabeth,' the feel of his hand on her hair touched her deeply, and she felt the tears well up, 'look at me, Elizabeth.'

With wide eyes she met his gaze. 'Lord Michael,' she whispered meekly, 'I'm so terribly sorry.'

'Yes, I'm sure you are,' he said, and the tears began to meander down her cheeks. 'But the most important thing is you made it back safely.'

'Will you ever forgive me?'

'Of course, but you deliberately disobeyed me, and you will therefore be punished.'

She gulped. Of that she'd had no doubt, and punished severely she was sure. Not that she deserved less, she recognised that, which is something she would not have done only a little time before.

'Take your hairbrush and get into bed,' he went on. 'You can brush your hair while you drink your tea.'

'Yes, sir.' She reached out and he embraced her, hugging her tightly, mostly from relief that she was indoors, dry and safe. She sniffled and coughed again, and he knew she was going to end up with a nasty cold.

'Come on, you bad girl, under the covers.' He helped

her up and into bed, and she shivered a little again and sneezed. 'Where do you keep your hankies?' he asked.

'In the top drawer of my dresser,' she told him, and he quickly found them, and gathered her hairbrush as well. He handed the items to her and she gratefully took them, immediately blowing her nose then bursting into another fit of coughing.

'Oh dear,' she said nasally, the tip of her nose getting redder and redder, 'I'm afraid I'm not feeling well at all.'

'No, I'm sure you're not,' he said sagely. 'We'll get some hot tea into you, that will help a little.'

He went to the tray and poured them both a cup, pleased to see it was still steaming, and put some cakes on a plate.

'Here you are,' he said, placing the cup and saucer on her bedside table, along with the plate of food. She picked it up and sipped. It was heaven. He sat on the edge of the bed, looking sternly at her.

'Now then, young lady, I'm not interested in any excuses,' he said. 'You were downright disobedient and just determined to have your own way, weren't you, Elizabeth?'

'Yes, sir,' she replied quietly, sniffling again.

'You're to stay in bed for the rest of the day. I'll have Grace bring you lunch on a tray, and then you are to sleep this afternoon. If you're a good girl I'll come up and have dinner with you.'

'Yes, sir,' she said sheepishly. 'Thank you, sir.'

'If you need anything just pull the cord. Otherwise, under no circumstances do I want to see you up and out of this bed.' He patted the mattress beside her hip. 'Is that clear?'

'Yes, sir,' she repeated, feeling well and truly

admonished.

'And rest assured, when you're better your bottom will be redder than your nose is now, and I'll use this hairbrush to make it so. However, that won't be your only punishment, so think about that as you lay here recuperating.'

'Yes, sir,' she said, having no doubt whatsoever that he meant what he said.

'Good. Now I'm going to change out of these damp clothes and get back to work. As soon as you've finished brushing your hair I want you to get some rest.'

'Y-yes, sir,' she stammered, 'and thank you, sir.'

Lord Michael nodded, then without another word he picked up his shoes and socks and left the warm bedroom.

And Elizabeth did indeed come down with a very heavy cold, and there were further complications caused by the foul weather; it caused havoc with the roads.

Her father sent word to Lord Michael, asking if he could stay on for the week. Getting back to the country might be tricky, and returning to London might prove equally so for him. Lord Michael, still concerned about Elizabeth's convalescing was more than pleased to do so. There was no business so urgently in need of his attention that he couldn't stay on a little longer.

After several days of bed and lots of good food and constant attention, Elizabeth woke up on the third morning feeling almost back to her old self. Lord Michael insisted on another twenty-four hours of rest, and as she had no intention of displeasing him again she did not protest, even though she was frightfully bored.

On the fourth day she woke up with a clear head, no sniffles, and her throat was no longer sore. She smiled happily as Grace pulled open the drapes and stoked the fire. She was better, but the weather had not improved at all. It was teeming with rain for the fourth day in a row.

As she sat up in bed, stretching, there was a knock on the bedroom door. 'Are you decent?' Lord Michael asked from out on the landing.

'Yes, decent and much better,' she called back, hurriedly running her fingers through her hair.

He entered and saw Elizabeth sitting up, smiling happily, her cheeks rosy with health, not fever. 'Excellent,' he said. 'You look much better, Elizabeth. The additional day was just what you needed to completely see off your nasty cold.'

'You were right, as usual, sir. I feel as bright as a button.'

'She does look the picture of health, sir,' said Grace, clearly as pleased as anyone that her mistress was no longer ill.

'Well, as you can see, it's still awful outside,' he went on, 'so when you're up and about I'll see you in the sitting room.'

'Wonderful,' she beamed, delighted she was finally going to be out of her sickbed.

She took her time getting ready, enjoying a long soak in the bath, then chose something particularly pretty to wear and pinned her hair up. Pleased with her appearance, she trotted down the stairs to the sitting room.

He was waiting for her, sitting on the sofa reading a book. 'Well, there she is, and doesn't she look lovely?' he said, looking up at her as she entered.

She blushed a little. 'Thank you, sir.'

'Come, sit,' he said, patting the cushion next to him, and she perched elegantly on its front edge as he held her hand. 'What would you like to do on your first day up and about?' he asked. 'Not that we can leave the house, of course; damned foul weather.'

So after a tasty luncheon they returned to the sitting room and spent the afternoon enjoying each other's company, playing cards and sharing stories about recent events.

However, as the day passed Elizabeth could not help but wonder when the inevitable would happen – when she would have to pay the price for her gross disobedience of the other day.

Her feelings of trepidation aside, the pleasurable hours skipped by quickly and soon they were chatting amiably over dinner, so much so that she began to wonder against hope that he had totally forgiven her, but just as she dared to believe that her worries were over he lowered the boom.

She had laid her knife and fork neatly together on her empty dinner plate, when he looked across the table and holding up his glass of red wine, said quietly, 'Elizabeth, take a good look at the wine in this glass. Do you see what a pretty red it is?'

'Um, yes sir,' she said carefully, sensing what was about to come.

'Well, that's close to the colour your beautiful bottom is going to be in about half an hour.'

She gulped; his tone was resolute and very stern.

'There will be no dessert for you this evening. Instead you will take yourself up to your bedroom, lay out five scarves, then take off all your clothes and lay yourself facedown on your bed. Remember, Elizabeth, I want you completely naked. I'll be up shortly, when I have enjoyed my dessert.'

She felt her face flush. She wanted to throw herself on the floor in front of him, beg him to let her off, but she knew it would not only be useless, he would consider her impudent and just add to her punishment quota.

Besides that her conscience was bothering her, and it was only after she had paid for her disobedience that she would be free of her guilt. That was one of the things he had quickly taught her, and taught her well. Bowing her head she stood up and humbly whispered, 'Yes, sir.'

She walked up the stairs to her bedroom, gathered the scarves he had ordered, laid them on the bed, and got undressed. When naked she then laid on the mattress to wait, knowing it might be five minutes, or ten, or twenty or more.

Lord Michael enjoyed a leisurely dessert; apple sponge cake with ice cream, and then enjoyed a nice cup of coffee. He knew Elizabeth would be waiting as he had ordered, full of trepidation, as she should be. He wanted her to think about just how headstrong and foolhardy she had been, and when well fed and ready he stood up and started up to her room. When he reached her door he pushed it open and entered quietly, noticing her tense slightly as she heard a slight sound, but she did not get up or speak or look in his direction. He closed the door, and then stood for a moment taking in the breathtaking vision before him.

The fire was the room's only light, and her lovely body was bathed in its golden glow. Her soft skin looked almost translucent, and her bottom cheeks rose provocatively.

Lord Michael set to work, and the first thing he did was slide some pillows under her stomach, raising her bottom perfectly. Then he tied her wrists and ankles to the four posts of the bed, and during the entire process Elizabeth did not speak, except to utter an uncertain whimper or two. Lastly came the darkest scarf of the selection she'd gathered for him, which he used to blindfold her.

He found the hairbrush on her dresser, and picking it up he slapped it down into his palm, seeing her flinch enticingly. Then sitting beside her on the bed he ran the smooth wooden back of the brush across the creamy contours of her elevated buttocks. A slight tremble ran through her delicious form.

'Are you ready for your punishment, Elizabeth?' he asked.

'Yes…' she whispered, 'yes sir, I think so, sir.'

'You know you deserve to be punished, don't you?'

'Yes sir, I do know that.' Her sweet voice was partly muffled by the bedspread.

'You are well aware of what you did wrong, so I won't waste any time reminding you of your disobedience. I am going to paddle you with your hairbrush, and you are going thank me for it afterwards, aren't you, Elizabeth?'

'Yes, sir,' she answered, her voice quavering.

'So, are you ready?'

'Yes, sir,' she quaked, gritting her teeth.

He raised the brush in the air, and with a practiced flick of his wrist brought it down on her right cheek, making her yelp as the flat wood burned her skin with a searing sting.

He repeated the action, and as he found his rhythm he watched with satisfaction as her porcelain-white flesh turned a gratifying crimson.

She clenched her teeth through the scorching smacks, determined to take her spanking with fortitude. She had brought it on herself, she knew, and deserved every stinging slap.

By the time he finished her bottom was bright red, radiating heat. He brushed his fingers between her legs. She was wet, and despite her smarting posterior she gasped with pleasure.

'You like that, don't you, Elizabeth?' he said.

'Oh, yes sir,' she breathed. 'I do like that…'

'It makes you forget about your stinging bottom, doesn't it, Elizabeth?'

'Yes, sir, it does help me forget a little.'

He continued to rub, his fingers moving against her clit, and she wriggled in response. He slid his thumb into her hot recesses, and she pushed back against him.

'Now then, Elizabeth, next time I tell you to do or not to do something, you will obey me, isn't that so?'

'Yes sir,' she replied huskily, 'in future I will always obey you, sir.'

His fingers kept massaging her. 'And you will always remember this evening, won't you?'

'Yes sir.' Her voice became more dreamy and her breathing more ragged.

'Good, and now I doubt you'll ride your horse comfortably for several days.'

'Yes sir, I'm sure you're right,' she agreed, and then suddenly caught her breath, signalling the onset of her moment. But he pulled his fingers away and she tensed, groaning in frustration.

'What's the matter, my dear?' he goaded, running the tips of his fingers across her inner thigh. She wriggled, her blotchy red bottom moving salaciously before him.

'Oh sir, I – uh – I…'

'You were going to orgasm, weren't you?'

'Yes, sir…'

'And do you honestly think you deserve such pleasure, after being so poorly behaved?'

She moaned into the bedspread, then panted, 'No sir, you're right, I don't deserve such pleasure after being so poorly behaved.'

'That would be correct,' he agreed, slipping his fingers back between her legs, rubbing again, his practiced hand causing her to writhe in her bonds, craving more, then as soon as he knew she was at the edge again he pulled his hand away once more.

'Oh, sir…' she wailed in disappointment, 'please don't be so cruel to me.'

'Elizabeth, I told you; you were not just going to be spanked,' he said calmly. 'You need to learn patience. It was lack of patience, in addition to your general wilfulness, that caused you to disobey me in the first place. Isn't that right?'

Her pussy was desperate for attention, her bottom sore and burning, but she was forced to pay attention to his words. Again he was right, the truth was on that fateful morning her impatience and petulance had gotten the better of her and she'd behaved poorly. 'Yes, sir,' she snivelled, 'that is right.'

'Good girl. Now you can just lay there and consider these things that you acknowledge for a while.'

'Of course, sir.'

Lord Michael moved to the chair by the fireplace and closed his eyes. A little after-dinner nap would be nice, and Elizabeth needed time to feel the heat of his discipline and ponder her waywardness. He felt a little sorry for her, for he had paddled her with severity, and she was now bound, blindfolded, wet, and aching for her orgasm, but she was in need of such discipline. Not only had she been disobedient, but the consequences of her disobedience had genuinely worried him.

He was not sure how much time had passed, but he suddenly woke with a start. He could not have been dozing for very long, he reasoned, because the fire looked much as it had when he nodded off.

He stood up, looking over at the bed. Elizabeth's mouth-watering bottom, still raised by the pillows, was very red and he could see her glistening pussy lips peeping from between her thighs, and the sight was naturally extremely inviting.

He stripped off quickly and she gasped as he knelt on the bed, between her parted legs, and lay across her back. His member was erect and ready, and he sandwiched his hands between her and the mattress, grasping her breasts. His fingers toyed with her nipples and she moaned, wriggling beneath him. He nuzzled her neck, just beneath her ear.

'Hello, Elizabeth,' he whispered. 'Have you learned your lesson yet?'

'Yes, sir,' she responded huskily. 'I have, I promise.'

'Do you deserve to be pleasured?'

'Only if you think so, sir.'

He kissed her neck and then knelt up between the triangle of her taut and shapely thighs, her bottom and sex raised by the pillows to the perfect level for his aims, his erection jutting powerfully from his shadowy groin. His fingers found her moist lips, spread them apart, and again she gasped and then moaned as his cock slid inside her. Then without hesitation he began to fuck her vigorously.

She cried out, muffling her pleasure by clamping her teeth to the bedcover, wanting to raise herself, to move against him, but her bonds held her tight. All she could do was accept him, but the restraint seemed to accelerate the onset of her orgasm and it only took a few minutes before she felt her moment arrive.

'Pluh-please sir,' she gasped, stunned at the suddenness

of her bodily response, 'm-may I?'

'No, you may not, and don't ask again,' he grunted savagely in time with his thrusts. 'You will wait until I say you can.'

'Y-yes, sir…' she sighed into the moving mattress.

He could feel her tight channel gripping him deliciously and he knew she desperately wanted to climax, but the little minx would just have to wait.

He continued to fuck her, mixing the power of his thrusts. He'd move slowly, then plunge quickly, and when he sensed she couldn't control her own hunger he remained completely still, teasingly squeezing her breasts or agitating her clit, until eventually the pleasure was too great to resist any longer and he was ready for his own release.

'Would you like to come now, Elizabeth?' he grunted into her ear.

'Oh yes, please sir,' she cried, then hastily added, 'if it pleases you, sir.'

'And you're going to show more patience from now on, as befits a demure young lady?'

'Yes, sir, I promise,' she wailed.

'Then you may come now, my dear,' he permitted, and increased his thrusts, tightly holding her hips. He plunged into her and she buried her face in the mattress to muffle her screams of joy. As her spasms took hold her pussy pulsated, sending him over the edge too, and he let out his own cries of carnal passion, exploding inside her. As much as her restrains would allow she rocked back and forth with him until they both collapsed. He felt his deflating penis slip out, but lay on top of her exquisite softness for a moment, catching his breath.

When a little more composed he rose from her warm

body and untied her ankles and wrists, then laid down next to her, removed her blindfold and pulled the covers over them. She snuggled close, resting her head against his chest.

'My sweet, naughty Elizabeth,' he murmured.

'Oh sir, I'm really very sorry for being so headstrong.'

'I should hope so. How does your bottom feel?'

She clenched her buttocks to judge fully how they did feel, and grimaced a little. 'Sore, sir,' she told him. 'Very sore.'

'Good. I hope it stays that way for a while.'

She cuddled even closer, and then raised herself on one elbow and looked into his eyes. 'Lord Michael?' she ventured, and then continued, interpreting his silence as permission to do so 'The spanking, and how you tied me up, and then, well…' as her voice tailed off she looked delightfully coy and uncertain, and decidedly embarrassed.

'Yes,' he urged, 'what of them, my dear?'

'Well…' she eventually continued, summoning her courage to talk of such brazen things, 'I just never felt… I mean… I just feel so… my heart feels so full. Is it permissible for me to say and admit that?' Her eyes were sparkling and her face was adorably flushed from her spent passions.

He smiled and pulled her back into his embrace. 'Yes,' he replied, 'of course it is permissible for you to admit that.'

Chapter Nine

Elizabeth's eyes fluttered open and she sensed it was early. Her sleepy gaze drifted around the room, and fell upon the discarded scarves lying over the chair by the fireplace. The memory of the night before sent a warm glow through her, as did the feel of the tender flesh of her bottom. Lord Michael stirred, and lying on his side, pulled her close, and as she snuggled back into his warmth his hands covered her breasts. What a delicious sensation, she thought, feeling his hardness pressing against her from behind. She eased her bottom back tighter against him, and closing her eyes she felt him slide into her. Not all the way, but just enough to tantalise her.

She waited for him to press deeper, but he didn't. Impatiently she wriggled a little, and his voice whispered in her ear, 'Be still, my sweet Elizabeth. Don't move.'

She held her breath and waited. His penis was sitting right at her entrance, teasing her dreadfully. She hungered for him, for the feel of his powerful length sinking inside her.

The minutes passed and his fingers began to toy with her nipples. He was driving her insane. She was desperate to move, or at least have him move, but he stayed perfectly still, resting there. Then he began to kiss and peck her neck, whispering husky endearments in her ear, her aching need increasingly becoming too much to bear and she instinctively ground back with her hips. He reacted quickly, pulling away, and holding her breasts firmly he said, 'What are you doing, Elizabeth? I instructed you to stay still. Now for your petulance you're going to have to wait even longer.' His fingers were still toying with her nipples and she moaned in frustration and at the foolishness of her impetuous behaviour.

'Yes sir,' she mumbled, 'it's just that I... I want to feel you inside me again so much.'

'And you would be doing so at this very moment, had you listened and obeyed. You always have to learn the hard way, don't you?'

She sighed. 'Sometimes it's just so difficult to be good, sir.' His fingers were still teasing her nipples, and then suddenly he pinched them tightly, a strident pain shooting through her. 'Ouch!' she cried, and he released his excruciating grip.

'I have to teach you about your beautiful breasts,' he whispered, 'and your naughty nipples.'

She felt her juices flowing and squeezed her thighs together. She didn't know quite what he meant, but the prospect of anything he had to teach her was hugely enticing.

His fingertips circled her pink cherries, tingling from the unexpected pinch, and then his hands moved down, between her legs, his fingers teasing her clitoris. She pressed against him.

'You're not getting anything more, Elizabeth,' he told her. 'You will learn to control your urges, and if you do not learn you will end up experiencing much frustration.'

She craved him, hoping against hope he would slide his fingers inside her, but instead he pulled back and began tracing his hand down her spine.

'And there is another area you must learn about, Elizabeth,' he went on, his voice monotone. 'It is another level of your surrender. It will show me just how sincere you really are about submitting to me utterly.'

'Oh, sir,' she gasped, 'please do not doubt my sincerity. I may be spoiled, and still somewhat obstinate, but I do *so* want to please you.'

'Pleasing me and complete submission are two very different things, Elizabeth. There are levels of surrender that you may or may not wish to explore.'

She didn't know what he meant. All she knew was that she could not imagine her life without him. Their voices fell silent, the early morning quiet broken only by the faint sound of a distant cockerel welcoming the dawn.

'I must away to my quarters,' he murmured.

'Oh,' she said, aching for his touch. 'I do so love waking up next to you, sir. I just wish…'

'I know what you wish, but you will have to wait. And as usual you have only yourself to blame.'

She sighed and rolled over to face him, giving him a quick cuddle before he left her bed. She watched him rise, partly dress, then quietly leave the room. Closing her eyes she tried to go back to sleep, but could not, the yearning need between her legs preventing any rest.

She wondered if she could find relief herself, but knew it would not be the wisest course of action. He had made it clear that he was in charge of her, completely, and he certainly had not told her he could satisfy herself. Just the opposite, in fact. So reluctantly she discarded the notion, and lay back in the dawn light, pondering his words.

By the time Grace appeared and opened the curtains Elizabeth was wide-awake. After days of confinement to her sickbed she was anxious to be up and about. She looked out of the windows and saw it wasn't raining. For the first time in days the sun was peeking between the clouds.

'Lord Michael thought you might be able to make it to town,' Grace announced, running her bath. 'He's waiting for you in the dining room. I told him I'd make sure you were down smartly.'

Elizabeth beamed. How wonderful! At last a day out! Hurriedly she took to her bath and then brushed her hair and dressed as quickly as she could. She then darted downstairs, anxious to join him, and found him as Grace had said, waiting in the dining room.

'Good morning, Elizabeth,' he said.

'Good morning, Lord Michael,' she replied, adding a little curtsy.

'Are you hungry?'

'I am, sir, yes,' she answered.

They sat at the dining table, and he watched his young charge ravenously devour her breakfast, and then ask for more. She had certainly made a full recovery, and he had to admit she looked as lovely as ever.

When they had finished their meal he ushered her into the sitting room, guiding her to the full bay windows.

'Grace mentioned a trip to town,' she said hopefully.

'Yes,' he confirmed. 'I am a little concerned about the roads, but it's not far and the road there was in excellent condition before the weather set in. I was just looking to see if the skies were threatening again, but I see the clouds breaking. I think we should give it a try. What do you think, my dear?'

She wanted to scream that she simply had to get out or lose her mind, that she wanted to mount her horse and gallop for hours, but instead she primly replied, 'If it pleases you, sir, I would love to go to town.'

He knew she was bursting to get out of the house and it must have been difficult to contain her natural exuberance, so he smiled approvingly. 'Good, then I shall have the carriage brought around.'

By the time Elizabeth was ready Lord Michael and the carriage were waiting for her at the bottom of the expansive front steps. Seeing her at the balustrade he strode up, and taking her elbow, guided her back down and opened the door for her. Gracefully she climbed in and took her seat, and felt immensely proud as he sat next to her.

The driver cracked his whip and the single horse moved off, and as they rode to town Lord Michael put a hand on her knee.

'Do you remember what we talked about early this morning?' he asked, 'about the different levels of surrender?'

'Yes, sir, I do,' she answered, feeling a flutter of nerves in her tummy.

'Did you understand what I meant?'

She felt a little embarrassed, because she hadn't – not completely. 'I have to admit, sir, I didn't quite, no.'

'Ah, just as I thought,' he mused. 'Not to worry though; you will.'

The promise secretly thrilled her, and she knew he was teasing, making sure her thoughts were exactly where he wanted them to be.

The town was full of life. People were bustling about, doing their best to avoid large puddles that had formed over the days of incessant rain. They were dropped near the main area of shops, making arrangements to meet the driver in two hours' time. If they needed the carriage before then, Elizabeth knew where the horse would be resting.

Taking his arm Elizabeth fell into step with Lord Michael, and they walked slowly down the busy street, not going anywhere special, just enjoying each other's company. As they passed an odd little shop Lord Michael stopped and looked in the window. It was full of bits and pieces; clocks, watches, ivory-backed brushes and combs; all manner of enchanting knick-knacks.

'Let's go in,' he suggested, and led her through the door, a little bell tinkling, announcing their presence. It was quite dim inside, and there was a distinct aroma of something Elizabeth could not quite identify. It wasn't unpleasant; in fact she quite liked it. They browsed quietly, eventually coming to a large glass case and they admired its myriad contents, Elizabeth spotting a charming silver case.

'Look, Lord Michael,' she said in hushed tones, as though they were in a library, 'what do you think that is?'

He peered down. It wasn't very large, and had delicate, ornate engraving.

'Can I help you?' The proprietor was an elderly man, thin and balding, with small round spectacles.

Lord Michael asked to see the case, and Elizabeth watched in fascination as the old man plucked it out and showed them how it worked.

It had four tiny doors. The two small ones at the top opened to reveal a round ball, and when the two larger doors below were opened the ball turned, playing a tune. It was a dear little music box, the interior lined with dark red velvet.

'Isn't it sweet?' she squealed excitedly. 'I don't think I've ever seen anything quite like it.'

'Yes, it is rather lovely,' Lord Michael agreed. 'Would you like to have it, my dear?'

A warm blush suffused her throat and cheeks. Her father was always buying her gifts, and there was almost nothing she could not ask for, but the offer from Lord Michael made her positively dizzy with delight.

'I – um – I don't quite know what to say,' she blustered.

'Generally speaking, since falling ill you seem to have learned your lesson and been a good girl,' he acknowledged. 'And when you're good you get rewarded.'

She felt her face turn crimson, both from the remark in front of the shopkeeper, and the stirring memory of what happened when she was naughty.

'So, would you like to have this little music box?' he asked again.

'I would be so proud to own it, sir,' she replied, barely able to speak.

'Excellent, then we shall take it, thank you,' he said, addressing the bespectacled man behind the old counter, and taking his wallet from his jacket he pulled out some notes. Elizabeth was so taken aback she didn't know what the merchandise cost, and didn't care. Whether it had been a shilling or a pound it would always be priceless to her.

The shopkeeper placed it carefully in a sturdy box, and handed it over to Lord Michael.

Elizabeth felt flushed and happy, and as they left she suppressed the overwhelming temptation to rise up on her toes and kiss him on the cheek. Such unladylike behaviour would not be appropriate in public, and now, more than ever, she wanted to be a very good girl indeed.

They walked around town for some time, Elizabeth stopping to greet those she knew, introducing them to her escort. After a while Lord Michael suggested a cup of tea, and Elizabeth was grateful to accept; her feet were becoming tired and a refreshing cup of hot tea would be rejuvenating.

They entered the tearoom, the only one in town, and Lord Michael found them a table near the window. A large woman waited on them, and he ordered tea and scones. After she waddled off he put the gift box on the table.

'Why don't you examine it more closely?' he offered.

Eager to do so, Elizabeth opened the present and withdrew the beautiful silver music box. She opened the little doors and marvelled at the intricacy of the engraving.

'It really is beautiful,' she sighed. 'Thank you so much, sir. It was very generous of you to buy it for me.'

'Not at all, my dear, I'm glad you like it. No matter what happens you shall always have that as a memento of our special time together.'

The words struck her. 'What do you mean, whatever happens?' she asked, panic rising from her stomach.

'Elizabeth, you've come such a long way in such a short space of time,' he said worryingly. 'You're a different young lady to the one you were just a few days ago, wouldn't you agree?'

'Yes, sir,' she admitted, 'I would agree.'

'And that may be all you wish for, but I told you about the layers of surrender, Elizabeth.'

'Yes, sir?'

'Well, if you do not wish to completely submit to me, in all the ways I require, then our journey must reach its end soon.'

She felt the colour drain from her face. What was he talking about? 'D-don't you care for me, sir?' she asked timorously, truly shaken.

'Of course I care for you, my dear,' he reassured her. 'But it's not about how much I care for you, it is about how much you care for me.'

'But I don't understand,' she stumbled, feeling a lump in her throat. 'I care for you deeply, sir. I have given you all of me.'

'Not quite,' he countered, his voice calm and even. 'There is more for you to learn, and I don't yet know whether or not you care to learn it.'

Elizabeth took a long deep breath, trying to quell the panic inside her. Then, with as much conviction and sincerity as she could muster, and looking him directly in the eye, she said, 'Lord Michael, please know that I want to learn absolutely everything you wish to teach me. Absolutely everything.'

He raised an inquisitive eyebrow. 'I do not doubt you feel that way now, but your certainty remains to be seen.'

The waitress was suddenly upon them with their tea, and Lord Michael watched as Elizabeth raised the delicate china cup from its saucer to her lips with a trembling hand.

'Don't worry, Elizabeth,' he said, attempting to reassure her. 'All will fall into place, one way or another. Just remember, ultimately it's up to you.'

The words eased her mind somewhat, and she recalled he had given her a choice once before, the night he tied her to the curtain rod. She sensed something similar was in store for her soon, but what could she offer that would be more of a surrender than her maidenhead?

Lord Michael artfully moved their conversation to matters light-hearted, and she began to relax. Then after they finished their tea they set out to enjoy the rest of their time in town.

In spite of his words she was encouraged by his manner. On more than one occasion he whispered salacious words in her ear, and by the time they climbed into the carriage to head home, she was feeling quite warm with need.

Once home he took her arm and led her to the sitting room.

'I suspect the tea and scones has dulled your appetite for further afternoon tea,' he surmised. 'Would that be correct?'

Elizabeth was still simmering with yearning, and the last thing on her mind was food. 'Yes sir, although I do have an appetite,' she ventured cheekily, 'but only for... for...'

He smiled. 'Yes, I know very well what you have an appetite for, young lady, but we shall now see how much of one, shall we not?

'Submission, Elizabeth; just how much are you prepared to submit?' He let the question hang in the air for a moment. 'Go to your room,' he finally continued, 'take a long hot bath, then wait for me on your bed, on your hands and knees, with a scarf covering your eyes. Any questions?'

Butterflies were fluttering in her stomach, but she managed to respond, 'No, sir, no questions.'

'Good. Off you go, then.'

Filled with dangerous, erotic anticipation, Elizabeth scurried up to her room and found Grace dusting. She ordered her to draw a bath and then to leave, and not to disturb her under any circumstances.

Grace could tell her mistress was in quite a state, and without a word she did as instructed. As soon as she had left Elizabeth took off and carefully hung her clothes in one of her large wardrobes, then sank into the hot water.

It was fragrant with rose scent, one of her favourites,

and she attempted to relax in the soothingly hot water. But it was impossible. She knew there was a test coming, a test of her devotion to Lord Michael, and she was determined not to disappoint him.

Lifting herself from the steaming water, she dried herself and dabbed some oil of rose about her body. She ran a brush through her hair, and could not help but recall exactly how that very same brush had been used to spank her. She quivered, and then felt herself grow moist between her thighs from the memory.

She applied a little rouge and lipstick, wanting to look as pretty as she could, then climbed onto her bed to wait. The minutes ticked by, the waiting agony. Then she remembered the scarf, found it quickly, and had just tied it in place when she heard the sound of the door opening. She froze, kneeling on the bed as instructed, praying she'd made it in time.

'Excellent,' Lord Michael said. He closed the door and turned the key. He certainly did not want any uninvited interruptions.

Elizabeth gasped as fingers touched her buttocks, and then lightly probed between her sex lips.

'Hush,' he said pre-emptively. 'Don't speak unless I give you permission.'

She nodded her head, wanting to obey him.

More fingers reached under her, pinching her nipples, which were already stiff from her hours of anticipation. He pinched again, harder, and she winced. Then she felt something cold and hard pressing against them. Whatever it was it grasped like his fingers, but the pinching was more intense and didn't cease. She felt him move away from her, but the pinching persisted. Whatever he had applied was grasping her nipples of its own accord. A throbbing pain began to permeate her breasts. She'd never felt anything quite like it – pain, but tormenting pleasure also.

'Listen carefully, Elizabeth,' he said. 'Do exactly as I tell you. If you hesitate I'll assume you don't wish to obey me any further and I shall leave. Is that clear? You may answer me.'

'Yes, sir,' she whispered.

'Good. Now lay your head on the bed and move your hands back, onto your bottom.'

It seemed an odd instruction but she did not hesitate, and immediately did as he asked.

'Now spread yourself for me. I wish to inspect you.'

A flash of humiliation swept through her. He couldn't possibly be serious, but then she remembered his warning.

He waited patiently, having already decided to count to three. If she hadn't done as he'd asked by then, her limits of surrender had been reached. He was silently at 'two' when her hands moved, and her sweet anus was revealed to him.

'What a good girl you are, my dear,' he mused. 'I'm very proud of you.'

Elizabeth was completely overwhelmed by the praise, the command, her humiliation, and the depth of her desire to please the severe gentleman.

'Levels of submission, Elizabeth,' he stated, and she remembered not to reply. 'I'm going to touch you there now,' he told her, knowing she would need a moment to emotionally prepare herself for such an intimate intrusion. As expected, he heard her gasp.

Removing a small jar of lubricant from his pocket he spread the greasy substance on his finger. He rubbed it against her, and then slid his finger just inside her tiny puckered entrance. She was moaning and sighing as he continued to toy with her, then slid his other hand down and began tickling her clit. She couldn't help herself, and wriggled in response.

'You're doing very well, Elizabeth,' he praised her again. 'Just sink into the delicious feelings my touch is inducing.'

His words helped, as did the insistent biting at her nipples and his knowledgeable fingers, but she was still overcome by the naughty probing in her bottom.

He could sense her reticence, her continuing confusion and chagrin. 'Feel, Elizabeth,' he quietly urged. 'Do not think, just feel.'

His coaxing was what she needed. Being led meant she was absolved of responsibility, and she began to accept the intrusive finger. The sheer debauchery of the situation was increasingly turning her on, and she ground her bottom back, inviting him to frig her.

'Ah, sweet Elizabeth,' he mused. 'Aren't you the little strumpet? Tell me what a little strumpet you are.'

Her bubble of joy was growing, becoming larger by the second. 'I'm your little strumpet, sir,' she sighed, the admission shooting sexual sparks through her body.

'Yes, you are,' he proclaimed, then abruptly withdrew his finger from between her cheeks, and his hand from between her legs. 'Kneel up, Elizabeth,' he commanded, 'and wait.'

She was weak from the experience and took a deep breath, attempting to gather her wits as she heard water running from the taps in the bathroom.

'You do look particularly lovely,' he said, returning and brushing a hand across her stomach, then around to her back. He gave her a sharp smack, first on one buttock and then the other.

'Elizabeth,' he continued, 'I smacked you not to punish you, but to get your full attention. You need to listen to me very carefully.'

'Yes, sir,' she replied.

'I am going to ask you a question, then explain something to you. First, do you know what it means to have a master?'

She thought carefully, wanting to please him with the correct response. 'Well, my father is the master of this house, and that means the servants have to obey him.'

'And if I were to be your master it would mean you obeying me, wouldn't it?'

'Yes, sir,' she said, feeling a little light-headed, her breasts pulsing from the nipple clamps.

'But I do not want to be your master unless you crave me to be,' he stated pointedly, manipulating her emotions. 'Not unless it is your absolute desire to submit to me, completely and utterly. So, do you want me to be your master, Elizabeth?'

'Oh, yes sir!' she cried without hesitation.

'Well then, we shall have to see if you really mean that, my dear girl. Perhaps one of these days you will have earned that right.' He moved his hands to her buttocks, pulling them apart, leaning down to kiss her neck. 'Are you my little strumpet?' he whispered in her ear.

'Yes sir, I am your little strumpet.'

'Then show me what a little strumpet you are.'

He released her and she put her face to the mattress, and placing her hands on her buttocks she spread them apart. He smiled, but didn't touch her there. Instead he placed his fingers against her clit, and rubbed vigorously until she was whimpering with need.

'Keep your hands where they are, little strumpet,' he

said, and from a pocket he withdrew a small artificial penis, much smaller than his proud member, but certainly big enough to begin the process of stretching her. He lubricated it well, and then touched it to her tiny entrance. She gasped, tensed, and then relaxed as he slowly pressed. 'What are you, Elizabeth?' he asked.

'Y-your little strumpet... sir,' she sighed, and then, as if wanting to prove her words, thrust back against the rude intruder.

As he worked the dildo between her cheeks he busied his fingers between her sex lips, and she accepted it, allowing it to completely invade her tight rear passage. Then holding the flange securely between thumb and finger he knelt behind her on the bed and placed his swollen erection at her pussy entrance. 'Do not move,' he ordered quietly but firmly.

She stayed completely still, almost fearing to breathe. The dildo inside her felt powerful, almost overwhelming, but she didn't feel any pain. A hand caressed her buttocks. It was so difficult not to move or utter a sound. She felt his hardness press between her pussy lips, lodging just inside her, and she felt it against the fullness of the intruder in her bottom. It was an odd but scintillating sensation.

He pushed in further, his cock filling her, and he began to fuck her. His movements were artfully languid, but firm and sure. Her nipples were aching sweetly and she could feel her orgasm growing. All day she had wanted this, all the time they wandered the town, her gloved hand demurely on his arm, she had secretly yearned for this whilst smiling politely at people they passed – people who would have no idea what naughty thoughts were in her head and sensations in her body.

'You have deserved your release, Elizabeth,' he said,

easing a hand between her legs.

'Thank you, sir,' she whimpered, aching for the moment.

'You may come, my little strumpet,' he permitted, 'and move as you wish.' Taking the flange of the dildo he began to stroke her, keeping the pace slow and firm, deftly in time with his own thrusts. She rocked back to meet him, wanting the feel of everything he was doing, her inhibitions abandoned. The bubble rose and suddenly exploded, and she cried as the spasms shook her. She felt her inner walls pulsate around him and then, just as suddenly, felt his glorious eruption as well.

He stiffened, clutching her hips, riding it out until finally he was spent and his wilting cock slipped from her, sucked completely dry of his manly essence.

She collapsed wearily on her front and he gently withdrew the dildo from between her bottom cheeks. He then went to the bathroom, cleaned up quickly, returned and instructed her to kneel, then removed her blindfold. She was still light-headed and when he told her to hold her breath she was puzzled, but did so, then quickly he removed the silver clamps from her nipples.

'Good girl, Elizabeth,' he said warmly. 'It just helps the pain to hold your breath and prepare for it.'

Her eyes were sparkling and she smiled up at him gratefully.

'Go and clean up,' he said, and swatted her rump to get her moving. 'I'll be right here when you have done so.'

She was exhausted, and all she wanted to do was take a nap, but dutifully she obeyed.

He stretched out on the bed, savouring the moment. She had done very well indeed. For years he had been searching for that one special female, but though many wanted to call him master, to date he'd found none truly worthy.

Chapter Ten

It was lunchtime. The weather was pleasant, the days of persistent rain having passed. Lord Michael had told her he would be busy all morning, so she spent the time riding her mare, albeit cautiously, across the wet fields.

'The ground will still be muddy in areas, and it's best to take things slowly for a few days,' he had warned, so she promised him there would be no fast gallops, and she had every intention of keeping that promise. Now she was sitting at the dining room table, waiting for him to join her for their midday meal.

'Elizabeth,' he said when he appeared, 'I want you to put together an overnight bag. Just a few changes of clothes and what little else you need. The very bare essentials, you understand?'

'Oh sir, how thrilling!' she squealed excitedly. 'Where are we going?'

'Never you mind where we're going. You'll find out soon enough. Be quick now; you've thirty minutes, and if you're not down here ready to go I'll leave without you.'

'Yes, sir!' she exclaimed eagerly, and he chuckled at her infectious enthusiasm.

They were soon on their way, seated in the carriage, moving along the road at quite a clip. Elizabeth could not imagine what he had up his sleeve. How did he gain her father's consent to take her away somewhere? But then,

116

she didn't really care. They were off on an adventure, and she could not have been happier.

They didn't travel very far, just to the railway station, and as they boarded a train headed north, she was thrilled at the thought of going on a journey with Lord Michael. He was carrying her overnight bag, and a steward showed them to their cabin, cramped but cosy. It was the first time she would spend the night on a train, and to do so in Lord Michael's arms – how simply wonderful and romantic!

The steward left them, and she pulled out the few dresses she had folded into the overnight bag, hoping the creases would fall out by the following morning. Lord Michael poured them a glass of champagne each from a waiting bottle, complements of the railway to their VIP customers, and as she turned to face him he held it towards her.

'Here you are, Elizabeth,' he said. 'This little excursion is a treat for your very good behaviour last night. Remember what I told you? Good girls are always rewarded.'

She took the glass, smiling merrily, and they clinked and sipped. A whistle blew and they heard the conductor's voice calling for the last minute passengers.

'Let's sit here by the window and have a look as we pull out, shall we?' Lord Michael suggested.

'Yes, sir,' she beamed. 'This is all such a lovely surprise. Thank you, so very much.'

He just smiled, and they settled in the chairs at the small table by the window.

The train chugged and rattled, and they watched in comfortable silence as the countryside rolled by, drinking their champagne, enjoying the anticipation of the pending

117

excursion. Then suddenly, and for no apparent reason, Elizabeth began to giggle.

'What on earth's the matter with you?' he asked. Elizabeth thought the question uproariously funny and burst into fits of laughter, and he realised, while she wasn't drunk she was quite tipsy, the bubbly champagne having gone straight to her head.

'Hmmm, enough of this for you I think,' he decided, removing the champagne glass from her hand.

She nodded in agreement, afraid that if she spoke she would slur her words or break into giggles again, but then the strangest thing happened; she yawned, a long deep yawn.

'My poor, Elizabeth,' he said, shaking his head. 'You really cannot cope with too much of this, can you?'

She looked at him a little bleary-eyed, and yawned again. 'I don't know what's the matter with me,' she managed. 'I'm so excited but all of a sudden I can hardly keep my eyes open.'

'Come, off with your clothes, let's take a little afternoon rest,' he suggested. 'Then we'll be fresh for dinner, and whatever else the evening brings.'

'Yes, I'd quite like to lay down,' she said, completely missing the implication of his innuendo. She stood up, but had to grab the table for support. 'I do seem to be having a spot of bother,' she said, and despite her abrupt tiredness, giggled again.

He held her by the arm to steady her. 'Here,' he said, 'I'll help you.' He undid the buttons at the back of her dress and pulled the garment down off her shoulders. Her milky skin appeared, and he marvelled at its satin sheen. He turned her around, catching a glimpse of her nipples pressed against the light silk of her petticoat, feeling

118

himself hardening and wanting to have her right there and then. But he led her gently to the narrow bunk and laid her down, stripped quickly, then stretched out alongside her. She snuggled up to him as if it was the most natural thing in the world.

He could smell the fragrance of her hair and skin, and she looked so peaceful and contented. He sighed deeply, closed his eyes, felt the rocking movement of the train, breathed her in one more time, and let himself drift off.

It was quite late, but the dining car was still almost full. They were shown to a table, and Lord Michael immediately ordered a second bottle of champagne. He then studied her in silence for a while.

'How do you feel, Elizabeth?' he eventually asked.

She smiled back at him, merriment in her eyes, her cheeks rosy. 'Fine, sir,' she said. 'That rest was just what the doctor ordered. I was feeling quite silly before that.'

He nodded sagely. 'Champagne will do that to you. Speaking of which...'

The waiter arrived with their glasses and chilled bottle, along with a basket of bread, and once alone again Lord Michael took her hands across the table. 'Elizabeth, in a minute I am going to sit next to you.'

'Oh, how nice,' she replied politely, not really thinking much of it.

'And put my hand under your dress,' he continued. She stared at him, not believing what she had just heard. 'Then I am going to caress your thighs.' Elizabeth felt herself turning red and nervously looked around the dining car to see if anyone else could hear him. 'Then slide my hand into your panties, and play with you.' She swallowed hard, wishing she could grab her champagne glass and

119

take a big swallow, but his hands were still clutching hers. 'When I feel you are about to climax I will stop, but ultimately you will have your orgasm right here at this table. Just remember, Elizabeth, when I finally allow your release, you must be utterly discreet. After all, we are in a public place.'

She still could not bring herself to speak.

'Elizabeth, do you understand what I just told you?'

She nodded dumbly, wishing to protest but knowing it was pointless, then without another word he stood and eased onto the seat next to her.

The waiter walked by, and she was sure he could see Lord Michael's hand moving on her knee, searching for a way into her skirt. Then it disappeared from view and she could feel it on her thigh, just above the tops of her stockings. Despite her angst she felt herself growing wet, and could not help but close her eyes, a tiny gasp escaping her lips. Suddenly she felt a sharp pinch and opened her eyes again, a little shocked at what he'd done.

He leaned close, his lips brushing her hair. 'That will not do, Elizabeth,' he said. 'You must keep your eyes open and make not a sound. You must behave as if nothing is going on. I will not tell you again. And if you do not obey me I will spank you right here, in front of everyone.'

She stared at him in disbelief. Would he really do such a thing? He was daring enough to be touching her in public, so yes, she was sure he really would do such a thing. She inhaled deeply and gathered her resolve.

'Yes, sir,' she whispered, and then took a shaky sip of champagne.

His fingers slid upward, finding their mark, and in spite of her self-consciousness she marvelled at how they made her feel. She gazed across the aisle at an elderly couple.

The man smiled at her. She knew her face was flushed, but smiled back, and felt a pinch just as she did so. Her expression froze; she wanted to flinch but she controlled herself, and did not make a sound.

His fingers began stroking again, tight between her thighs, seeking and finding her clitoris, and she felt a rush of sexual energy suffuse her body. It was indeed thrilling for him to be doing such things to her in public. She let out a sigh of adoration, for Lord Michael truly was the most daring of men.

He was enjoying himself immensely. The feel of her succulence was delicious, he could sense her excitement building, and just as the waiter arrived to take their orders he sank a finger into her.

'What would you like, my dear?' he asked, as if it were the most natural thing in the world to be doing what he was doing whilst giving their order. She tried to remember what she had decided upon, but couldn't recall. All she could think about was the most astonishing sensation of him touching her so intimately whilst in such close proximity to so many obliviously unaware people.

'Elizabeth, what would you like to order?' he repeated, beginning to withdraw his finger, and the unspoken threat of a public spanking inspired her voice.

'I-I was just trying to decide between the s-salmon and the ch-chicken,' she blurted, hoping both were on the menu.

'Well, the salmon is particularly good,' the waiter endorsed.

'Two salmon, then,' Lord Michael decided, for which Elizabeth was immensely grateful because his skilled finger had lost her the use of her vocal chords once again.

By the time the waiter arrived with their meal Elizabeth

was in quite a state of fluster, but Lord Michael withdrew his hand anyway and resumed his seat on the opposite side of the small dining table.

'Sir…?' she whispered desperately, left hanging on the brink.

'Eat your meal, young lady,' he said uncompromisingly. 'And you will receive a spanking later for such inappropriate behaviour. You should know better than to beg like a common whore.'

'Yes, sir,' she replied dejectedly, sorry for her conduct but mortified by the severity of his words, 'I'm sorry, sir.'

The meal was eaten with an uncomfortable silence between them, Lord Michael fully aware that his beautiful young companion had an admirer in the elderly gentleman sitting nearby with his equally elderly wife.

Once the agreeable food had been allowed to digest for a while, Lord Michael enjoying a cigar and a glass of brandy while Elizabeth sat respectfully quiet, he rose, offered his arm, and escorted her out of the rocking dining car to their compartment. Once inside he did not turn on any lighting, but closed the door and turned her to face him. 'Elizabeth, you are to be spanked, do you remember?' he said in the darkness.

'Yes sir, I remember.'

'First I have a quick errand to run, but when I return I want you naked and kneeling on the bunk, head bowed, hands behind your back. Is that clear?'

Elizabeth wanted to ask where he was going, but dared not. He watched her drop to her knees, and then leaving her in the submissive posture he slipped out of the cabin, hoping he was not too late to instigate his plan.

Upon returning to the compact cabin, task successfully accomplished, Lord Michael found Elizabeth obediently kneeling on the bunk, her toned body fighting the inconsistent movements of the train. She uttered not a sound as he settled in the small chair by the table, watching her, thinking how lovely she looked in the shadowy darkness.

'Stand,' he eventually ordered, and rose from his chair, telling her to close her eyes. She did so, knowing the blindfold was coming, feeling her excitement building again. She felt a soft fabric across her eyelids.

'This is a new blindfold for you, Elizabeth,' he told her gently. 'Do you like the feel of it?' She nodded. 'Good girl. Now, hands in front of you.' Obediently she obeyed, and felt silken ties bind her wrists together.

'Stay still,' he instructed, and she did. Then there was a hand on her neck and she was pulled down across his knees. There was a breathless pause, when the only sound in the cabin was the train rattling along the track, and just when Elizabeth relaxed a little and wondered what would happen next, his palm swept down and smacked her vulnerable bottom. She yelped as much from the shock as the pain, and then he spanked her again and again until she was squirming and writhing on his lap.

Her bottom was scalded and stinging, but she moaned with desire as she felt him touching her again, teasing between her wet pussy lips. He toyed with her a while until she was panting from need, as opposed to the smarting smacks of his palm. When the punishment was considered concluded he helped her up, guided her to the narrow bed, and placed her on all fours again.

The rocking of the train, the sound of the distant puffing engine, and the wheels on the rails beneath them created a converging mass of rhythms that strangely excited her. He wasted no time, and placing his erect member between her pussy lips he thrust and began fucking her avidly, skilfully utilising the motion of the train to deliver immense pleasure to them both. He clutched her hips and she cried out from the sheer pleasure of it all, but he then stopped fucking her abruptly, pulled out, and just waited at the entrance to her cunt.

'Do you want more?' he asked, his voice husky.

Despite her adoration of the man Elizabeth, her mind and emotions in turmoil, considered this an utterly stupid question and wanted to scream the obvious affirmative, but she knew better and instead replied with as much decorum as she could muster, 'If... if it pleases you, sir.'

A finger touched her tiny puckered entrance and she welcomed it. She didn't cringe or tense, or pull away. Rather, she salaciously sought it and he did not disappoint, sinking the straightened digit deep and frigging her, simultaneously thrusting his erection into her until his groin slapped noisily against her spanked buttocks.

She cried out, craving more, feeling her bubble build. She expected him to stop again but he didn't, and she quickly found herself on the brink awaiting his command to climax, and at last, when she was sure she could no longer control herself, she heard the words she was hungering for.

'You may come, my dear girl,' he grunted, his own passions threatening to simmering over.

She cried out in delight and came, feeling him do the same moments later, her bottom grinding lewdly back against him until finally their mutual shuddering dissipated. He let himself slide from her clinging wet warmth. She was flopped wearily on her stomach before him, and in the darkness he watched her languidly roll over onto her back. He untied her wrists, removed the blindfold, then laid next to her, wrapping his legs around hers, feeling her surrender to his arms.

'My little strumpet,' he said warmly, pulling her close.

'Yes sir,' she sighed contentedly, 'I am your little strumpet.'

'You're showing a lot of promise, Elizabeth.'

'Thank you, sir.' She yawned, already succumbing to the creeping fringes of sleep.

He listened to her even breathing, feeling deeply satisfied; things were moving along very nicely. As he let himself drift off too he thought about the things he had planned for his young supplicant, and he had to admit, he felt rather optimistic about them.

As the train pulled into their destination stop it was met by sunny skies, which matched Elizabeth's mood. She looked out of the window, sighing happily. The journey had already been more than she could have dreamed. She had been woken by Lord Michael fucking her from behind, and when that wonderful moment arrived her orgasm was a series of gentle waves that left her tingling and breathless.

He emerged from the tiny bathroom and saw her gazing wide-eyed at the early morning hustle and bustle on the station platform. He placed his arms around her shoulders and she melted back into his chest. There was no doubt they were extremely comfortable in each other's company, which was a pleasant and surprising bonus to him, considering the age gap.

Twenty minutes later he instructed the carriage driver of their required destination, and then again admired Elizabeth's shapely figure as she climbed up and settled in. He sat opposite her, and with a languid flick of the whip and a few clucking noises from the driver, the carriage moved off.

Elizabeth's curiosity was working overtime, and in no time at all it got the better of her, as he knew it surely would. 'Please sir,' she said, simply unable to contain herself, 'exactly where we are going?'

'You'll see,' he answered dismissively, and her sigh was followed by a tut. 'Excuse me?' he said, not having missed the instinctively impertinent reaction.

'I'm sorry, sir,' she said hastily, recognising her petulant response. 'I'm just curious. I simply want to know where we are going. I don't know why I can't—'

He cut her off with a look of steely menace. 'Elizabeth, I have arranged something for you, but in addition you are now going to be punished for that outburst. I do not appreciate the tone of your voice and persistent questioning of my plans, and it would appear that you are being impatient and impertinent once again despite my previous words and efforts. Am I wasting my valuable time on you after all?'

Elizabeth felt her face flush and the severe disappointment of disappointing him. She had let him and herself down again. He considered her impatient and impertinent, and now her bottom would pay the price.

'Now, you are to remain ladylike and quiet for the duration of the short last leg of our journey,' he ordered sternly. 'Do you think you can manage that?'

The sarcasm questioning her resolve hurt her, but she nodded demurely, and uttered not another word.

Eventually Elizabeth glanced out of the carriage window and spied the frontage of a modest but lovely old home.

They drove up the short drive and came to a halt in front of it, and the driver hopped down and opened the door for them. Lord Michael paid the man, then carrying their bags he led the way to the front door.

To her surprise he did not use the iron knocker, but set one of the bags down and opened the door. Entering the house Elizabeth gazed around, and broke into a broad smile. It appeared to be beautifully furnished, through an open door she could spy a welcoming fire burning in the sitting room to the right, and the aroma of spicy cooking filled the air.

Just then a robust, red-cheeked, grey-haired woman bustled into the hall.

'Lord Michael!' she beamed. 'How are you? It's been too long.' Her Scottish accent was broad, and Elizabeth could barely understand her.

'Hello, Millie, how's my favourite housekeeper?' He leaned down, pecking her on a ruddy cheek, and she laughed merrily.

'Oh, Lord Michael, you haven't changed at all. Lunch will be ready at twelve midday, sir, just as you ordered, then you'll have the place to yourselves.'

He nodded his satisfaction of her efficiency. 'Elizabeth, this is Mrs O'Grady,' he introduced them. 'Millie, this is my charge, Elizabeth Barrett.'

'Pleased to meet you, I'm sure,' the rotund lady boomed heartily. 'Lord Michael knows where you can rest up and have a bath after your journey.'

'Thank you,' Elizabeth answered politely. 'It's lovely to meet you.'

'I'll leave you to it, then,' Millicent went on. 'I mustn't let anything burn.' She waddled away.

'Come along, Elizabeth,' Lord Michael said brusquely,

and as he led her upstairs she could not take her eyes off the portraits adorning the walls.

'May I ask, sir, who lives here?' she ventured.

'This house belongs to a good friend of mine,' he informed her, 'Sir Andrew. He doesn't actually live here, he just uses it as a getaway and he was happy to lend it to me for a short break, along with Millie's fabulous cooking.'

'How kind of him,' she remarked. 'He must be a very nice man.'

Lord Michael smiled to himself. Yes, he was a very nice man. He was also a very strict man. They went along the short landing and stopped at a heavy oak door, which he opened grandly. The bedroom was lovely, with thick rugs on the floors, a fire burning, heavy red curtains at the windows, and most importantly, a four-poster bed with a canopy, boasting yards of fine drapery.

'Oh, Lord Michael!' she squealed animatedly. 'What a beautiful room!'

'Yes, it is indeed,' he concurred. 'And we are going to make full use of it, I assure you.'

Later, after a hearty lunch that was as delicious as he knew it would be, Lord Michael checked his pocket watch as he made his way downstairs. It was three-twenty, and Oliver Chadwick would be arriving in ten minutes. He made his way to the sitting room and poured himself a brandy, settling by the fire, warm and comfortable.

He thought about how well Elizabeth was responding to his training. She was a natural submissive, but so full of herself this hidden side to her had to be unearthed carefully. He had to admit he found her high-spirited nature amusing, and it did make things very interesting.

A knock at the front door broke into his thoughts, and knowing Mrs O'Grady had finished for the day, he moved to answer it. Oliver Chadwick, the elderly gentleman from the train, stood in the porch, holding a leather briefcase and looking quite flushed with anticipation. Lord Michael ushered him into the sitting room, offered him a brandy, which was accepted, and the two men sat comfortably by the fire.

'Mr Chadwick,' Lord Michael began.

'Oliver, please,' the older man insisted.

'Oliver…' the host nodded almost imperceptibly and smiled congenially, 'I shall waste no time in reaching the point. I must assume I guessed correctly, that you are a participant in the art of the rod, and the training of recalcitrant women?'

'Yes, sir, I most certainly am,' the man acknowledged, 'and should I assume the young lady with you on the train is in the process of her education?'

'Indeed she is. Her name is Elizabeth, and she is quite a handful.'

'Ah,' the man mused, 'Emily was like that. Still is from time to time, but I've always found the spirited females the most rewarding.'

'I would have to concur. I must warm her bottom and keep her needy a great deal of the time. Speaking of which, I asked you here today because that is exactly what's in store for her this evening, and I thought you might like to view the proceedings.'

'I would be delighted, dear fellow. I'm most flattered. As a matter of fact, anticipating such an invitation I have brought something with me. You may find it quite effective.'

'Really? How very decent of you. Please, Oliver, I am

most intrigued.'

Chadwick lifted the small case onto his lap, opened it, produced a beautiful riding crop and handed it to Lord Michael.

'Oh, how very handsome,' the recipient said sincerely as he turned it reverently in his hands, for it truly was a fine example of a master craftsman's work. The tip splayed into a number of leather strips, each one knotted at the very end.

'Custom made,' Chadwick announced proudly. 'Doesn't cut the skin or leave marks, but it carries a considerable sting which fair takes the breath away and quite some time to ease.'

'Oliver, this is indeed perfect for this evening's session,' Lord Michael said appreciatively. 'Elizabeth was quite misbehaved at times today. And whilst I gave her a few good smacks earlier, she has to learn that she will not be let off so easily if she persists in letting her standards slip. This is just the ticket, thank you, dear chap.'

Chadwick was elated; he was to see the employment of his favourite instrument of discipline on the cheeks of a delicious young lady – the very same young lady he had lusted after so recently on the train without ever imagining his secret fantasy involving her would ever actually come true.

'There's just one problem,' Lord Michael said, furrowing his brow. 'Whilst it will afford me great pleasure to share this evening with a gentleman so obviously a connoisseur of the art of discipline, I don't think Elizabeth is quite up to an audience just yet, so at the risk of offending my guest, I will have to ask you to observe in secret.'

Chadwick nodded his understanding.

'Elizabeth is blindfolded, waiting upstairs on the bed,' Lord Michael explained, 'and as my welcome guest you may sit quite comfortably and watch the proceedings. But before we venture further,' he continued, a glint in his eye, 'if you would give me your contact information in London, I'm sure other opportunities will arise, and as the girl accepts her submissive station over time I am sure you will be able to partake in her training in due course.'

Oliver Chadwick reached into his breast pocket and withdrew his card. He handed it to Lord Michael, an ebullient smile on his face. 'Any time, sir,' he said knowingly. 'I would be honoured to assist and offer any experiences that may be beneficial to you in the girl's training at any time you think appropriate.'

Lord Michael placed the card in his pocket, and then carrying the crop, showed Chadwick up the stairs.

When they entered the bedroom even the host caught his breath. Elizabeth looked positively breathtaking. Her naked and supine body was bathed in the warm, flickering firelight, legs parted as she'd been previously told to remain, bound hands on her tummy, blindfolded, her nipples pert and her curly bush glistening from her hunger.

Chadwick feasted his eyes as Lord Michael placed a chair at the foot of the bed, but to one side. It would give him the best possible view. He gestured for his guest to sit down, and quietly the elderly man did so, looking almost dizzy from the vision of the voluptuous submissive lying before him.

'Hello, Elizabeth,' Lord Michael said, looming over her vulnerable form. 'Have you had enough time to think about how best you can please me?'

The unseeing girl moved her head in the direction of the

voice, and hesitated a moment, running the unexpected question through her mind. 'To obey you, sir, in all things,' she eventually whispered.

He nodded with satisfaction. 'Very good, my dear, but you haven't exactly done that today, have you?'

She gulped, her lips glistening moistly in the firelight. 'No, sir, I suppose I haven't.'

'I know how much you want to enjoy an orgasm,' he said bluntly, 'and I know if I do this…' Lord Michael moved his hand between Elizabeth's legs, teasing her, and Chadwick heard her longing sighs, but she did not ask for release. It was clear she knew she would only have her moment when her tormentor decided. He nodded approvingly.

'I know I spanked you earlier today, but that was just an appetiser,' the standing man went on. 'Now you will be properly punished for not obeying me as you should have.'

Elizabeth groaned, aching to rub her thighs together, and wondered exactly what that punishment would involve.

'Up and over on all fours, Elizabeth, and move down the bed a little.' She struggled up on her hands and knees and edged backwards as Lord Michael took up his position, the long crop at the ready, and as she reached the foot of the bed he ordered her to stop.

He caressed her bottom with his free hand. The touch made her sigh, then he drew his hand back and the sound of a loud smack resounded about the room. Elizabeth yelped, his hand rose and fell again, and again she yelped.

Chadwick leaned forward a little and peered at the perfect red smudge of a handprint adorning her lovely bottom. Lord Michael glanced at him, and knew the old man was thoroughly enjoying himself. 'Are you ready for the next stage of your punishment, Elizabeth?' he asked.

'Yes, sir,' Elizabeth replied fearfully, wondering what would follow.

Lord Michael gripped the crop even tighter. 'Now then,' he said, his voice firm, 'is there a reason why you continue to lapse into disobedience, despite my time and efforts to eradicate such waywardness? Is there something wrong with your hearing, perhaps?'

'N-no, sir,' she stammered. 'There is nothing wrong with my hearing. Sometimes I just... I just think too much.'

'From now on, Elizabeth, you will obey first,' he insisted, 'and if you must think, you will do so secondly. Is that clear?'

'Yes, sir,' she said meekly. 'Obey first, think second.'

'Good girl. Now, I have something here that will help impress that lesson upon you in no uncertain terms. The sting you will feel is not one you've experienced before.'

'I'll be good, I promise,' Elizabeth murmured, feeling goose bumps crawl across her bare flesh.

'Yes, you will,' Lord Michael said sternly. 'Now be quiet and take your punishment.'

Stepping back, he traced the knotted leather tips of the crop across Elizabeth's bottom. He glanced at Chadwick, who gazed intently at the placement of the stinging ends, then nodded. Taking his cue, Lord Michael began flicking his wrist, making the switch whistle in the air, swishing it back and forth. It accelerated rapidly and Elizabeth started crying out, wriggling her bottom as the crop worked its magic. He watched as her bottom began turning a gratifying scarlet, and he did not have to whip her for very long for it was, as Chadwick had claimed, a very effective instrument indeed.

Interrupting the beating for a moment, Lord Michael moved closer and ran his fingers over Elizabeth's red and welted flesh.

'Oh, that stings so much!' she cried, the two men exchanging a knowing glance. 'I'll be so good, sir. I'll be totally obedient, I promise.'

'That is the general idea,' Lord Michael mused. 'Your obedience, or you suffer the subsequent punishment. I think that's easy to comprehend.'

'Yes, sir, my obedience at all times,' she cried again.

Her crimson flesh was indeed very hot, and he waited a moment then slipped a finger inside her. She groaned and he continued to tease her, bringing her to the edge, all the while stroking her scalded bottom.

He looked over at his elderly companion, and offered him the whip. Chadwick raised his eyebrows in surprise and delight, and standing, took the exquisite instrument. Lord Michael stood to the side, giving the elderly man plenty of room.

Chadwick stepped forward and ran the tips of his fingers across Elizabeth's tensed buttocks, eliciting a delicious hiss of breath from her parted lips.

'One more session with this marvellous instrument of discipline, and in future you will be obedient, won't you, Elizabeth?' Lord Michael said sternly, watching his cohort enjoy Elizabeth's charms.

'Yes, sir,' she whimpered, unsuspecting, tensing her bottom.

'No matter what the circumstances?'

'Yes sir, just obedience.'

The stinging of the whip had eased somewhat but her skin was still on fire, and as Chadwick adjusted his position slightly, laying the dangling leather strands against her buttocks, Elizabeth gripped the bedcover tightly in readiness.

He began to flick the ends back and forth, very lightly and slowly. Elizabeth squirmed. The slower action caused a sting and an itch at the same time. She was shifting her cheeks in a most lascivious manner, almost as if inviting his discipline. He increased the speed of the tormenting whip, and splicing it through the air with a degree of skill borne from hours of use, he brought it across her posterior in all manner of artful angles.

The man's talent impressed Lord Michael. The knotted tips could not be seen for the alacrity with which they moved, and the whip was horizontal one second then vertical the next. Elizabeth was squealing and writhing, but the hissing whip ignored her cries and continued its merry dance across her raised hindquarters.

Then gradually Chadwick slowed the punishment, making it tickle rather than sting, and moving closer still, slipped it between Elizabeth's pussy lips. She gasped and writhed desperately, her wails of pain becoming desperate pleas for release as he slid the crop deeper into her.

Elizabeth could hardly bear it. Her bottom felt like a thousand bee stings, and her pent up orgasm filled her with frustration. She pushed back, trying to make the teasing more substantial, but it made no difference. She moaned into the mattress, desperate for relief.

Clearly pleased with the girl's responses, the old man withdrew the crafted implement and handed it back to Lord Michael.

'Have I made my point?' he asked, replacing Chadwick and teasing her glistening wet sex lips with his crafty fingertips.

'Yes, definitely sir,' she gasped. 'Most definitely.'

'Good.' He slid his fingers into her, frigging her for a moment and coaxing her clit. She moved against him, her body aching for attention and release.

Chadwick returned to the chair. It had been several years since he'd had the pleasure of whipping such a fine young bottom, and he'd enjoyed it immensely. The feel of the strict rod as it danced its discipline upon her wriggling behind was tremendously fulfilling, and so with an erection the likes of which he'd not managed in recent memory, he was happily watching the gorgeous girl being teased. She was on fire, her body betraying its dark desires.

Lord Michael, satisfied with her desperate sighs, ordered her to move forward a little. He then stripped quickly, and as he climbed behind her, cock in hand, he noticed Chadwick extricating his own stiff penis from his trousers.

He smiled knowingly, and then holding Elizabeth's hips he placed his bloated tip at her glistening wet entrance, sank into her hot tunnel, and began to fuck her avidly. He moved his taunting thumb to her rear entrance and she mumbled incoherently, pressing back against his hand and onto his cock. She'd been held at bay for so long she was quickly at the brink, but Lord Michael was not yet ready.

He fucked her powerfully, watching her beaten red cheeks squirm before him, pushing back, asking for more, and every now and then he'd reach down to tickle her clit, keeping her on the very edge.

'Do you recall lying here, waiting for me, Elizabeth?' he asked through clenched teeth, ploughing into her, feeling his moment building. 'Do you recall aching for my erect cock inside you?'

'Yes... yes sir,' she gasped deliriously. 'I was desperate for you, aching for your erect cock inside me.'

'And now?' he coaxed. 'What are you craving now, Elizabeth?'

'To come, sir,' she sighed, then quickly added, 'but only if it pleases you, sir, if you think I deserve it.'

'That's what I like to hear, my dear,' he grunted, beads of sweat forming on his brow and at his temples. 'And so in that case...'

He thrust deeply home, accelerating his increasingly ragged movements, and then told her that she could come as she chose. She rode the wave, felt it rising inside, and moments later it crashed over her, leaving her panting and spent. She lay still as he continued to thrust, feeling her cunt tight around him, and suddenly he erupted, groaning loudly as he let himself go.

He rested a moment, and then let himself slip out of her wondrous confines. He looked over at Chadwick. The man was red-faced, breathing heavily, his shrivelled penis still in his hand, the cream from his orgasm seeping over his inert fingers and soaking into the handkerchief he'd spread over his lap to protect his suit.

'My dear fellow, what a splendid instrument,' Lord Michael gratefully praised his accomplice, a little time later as he showed him to the front door. 'Thank you, sir, for sharing it with me.'

'Lord Michael, the thanks are all to you,' Chadwick said enthusiastically. 'I've not had an evening like this in many years. I shall have one of these made for you,' he added as he carefully returned his crop to his case.

'That's most generous,' Lord Michael said gratefully. 'I shall be in touch upon my return to London.'

'I'll be looking forward to it,' Chadwick replied, and then thanking him again, shook his hand and left.

Lord Michael locked the front door and started back up the stairs. The chance meeting with the old master had proved to be far more satisfying than he could have hoped for, and he had no doubt the elderly gentleman could prove to be a veritable fountain of corporal punishment knowledge in the future.

He entered the bedroom, quickly got undressed again and climbed into bed. Embracing the weary Elizabeth he removed her blindfold, and she curled up, snuggling against him.

'How's your bottom, my dear?' he asked comfortingly.

'Stinging, sir,' she whispered ruefully. 'Really stinging.'

'Your obedience or a punishment, yes?'

'Yes sir, I understand. I'll be so good you won't have any cause for complaint. None whatsoever, I promise.'

He smiled to himself. Though she meant every word, he knew it would not be long before her bottom would once again be subjected to his discipline.

On the last morning of their brief break Lord Michael was the first to stir. He gazed at Elizabeth, admiring her beautiful face and tousled hair. She had woken something in him for which he'd long been searching. Every challenge he presented her with she not only undertook, but also embraced. He was extremely pleased with her. He glanced at the clock. It was already past eight and time to rise.

He kissed Elizabeth's forehead, whispered it was time to wake up and rise, then got out of bed and went to the bathroom. He started a bath for her, took care of his own needs, and then returned to the bedroom where she was still under the covers.

'Come along, my dear,' he told her. 'You have some work to do before we head back to the station. Meet me downstairs.'

She sighed and yawned prettily, but then smiled up at him and did as she was told. Finding the bath ready she bathed, then dressed quickly and made her way downstairs. She found him in the dining room, the remains of his breakfast on the table before him.

'Mrs O'Grady has the day off, dear girl,' he stated. 'I therefore want you to clean up the table and stack the dishes in the scullery.'

Elizabeth eyed the dirty plates and cutlery, but his training stood her in good stead, especially her recent whipping, and she immediately found her way to the kitchen. He strolled in behind her and put the kettle on to boil, so as to make them some tea.

She set about her chores quietly and diligently, scraping any scraps into old newspapers she found, and then folding them into a neat package. The food she felt could still be eaten she covered with clean brown paper and placed it in the pantry.

With the dining room table cleared she washed the crockery and cutlery and stacked them in the sink. Lastly, she found a clean cloth and gave the table a good wipe over.

Lord Michael watched with a sense of triumph. Not once did she complain, or whine, or suggest that she was too good for such menial work, and when she was finished he passed her the cup of tea he had actually made for them, the gesture of great significance to her because gentlemen of his standing simply did not do such things. She was proud of herself and the job she'd done, but even more so when it was obvious that he was happy with her too.

In the sitting room, drinking their tea together, her bottom

139

still glowing from the nights before, she felt enormously content.

It wasn't long before it was time to leave, and Lord Michael walked her back upstairs to gather their things. He reminded her to check that she'd not forgotten anything, and instructed her to make the bed. This too she did obediently as he packed his own bag.

And so it was she found herself in a carriage heading back to the train station, and she felt a little sad, for after such a short stay they were already headed home again.

And it was an even more dejected Elizabeth who stepped elegantly down from the carriage outside her home, for she could see her father's carriage in the yard. He was back, and that meant Lord Michael would soon be leaving them. How would she ever be able to stand it without him?

The man of her thoughts took her arm and guided her up the steps to the house. He talked to her in low tones, telling her he expected her to behave in a polite and gracious manner. She was to be respectful to her father, polite to her brother, and considerate to the servants. Her stomach knotted and her face flushed, as the familiar warmth spread between her legs, and she wished he were taking her up to her room to do all manner of unspeakably wonderful things to her.

She let out a deep sigh, and when her father met them in the hallway she bobbed, said hello respectfully, and told him how much she had missed him. Her brother, coming down the stairs, raised his eyebrows in surprise at her gracious manner.

The four of them enjoyed an agreeable lunch and Elizabeth remained on her best behaviour throughout, but all the while she could not stop thinking that Lord Michael would soon be leaving them, and it wasn't an easy task to remain cheerful.

After lunch the men disappeared into the drawing room, and Elizabeth took herself to her room, pondering what she might do to ease her feelings of despondency.

She sat at her dresser, running a brush through her hair. The very same brush he had spanked her with when she recovered from her heavy cold. How she wished she were over his knee at that very moment, her buttocks turning cherry-red under the smarting smacks of his hand.

She was embarrassed that this was what she yearned for, but alone with her thoughts there was no reason to be coy or untruthful. She didn't know why she ached for his discipline, but she just did.

Sighing, she laid the hairbrush down and flopped on her bed. No doubt he would be off to London in the morning, and she was very deflated by that prospect indeed.

A knock on her door made her jump, and thinking it was Grace she called for her to enter. But it was not the maid it was Lord Michael. She caught her breath, and was about to rush to him when he held up a warning hand. The house was full again, and such behaviour was no longer permitted.

'Since you've been such a good girl,' he said, entering the room but leaving the door ajar, 'I've convinced your father to allow you to join me for dinner in London, tomorrow evening.'

Elizabeth stood up excitedly. 'Oh sir, how wonderful!' she squealed in delight. 'Thank you, sir, so much!'

'Now, now, settle down,' he warned. 'Ladylike behaviour at all times, if you please.'

She took a deep breath and attempted to control her glee.

'We'll have a very pleasant time together, I'm sure,' he went on. 'Now pay attention.'

She thought about letting out another squeal of delight, just to ensure a spanking took place during the following evening.

'Your father was very impressed with your countenance at lunch, and believes my company is doing you the world of good.'

'Oh, sir, if only he knew,' she giggled mischievously.

'Elizabeth!' he barked, and immediately she settled herself down.

'Now, as I was about to say, I'll be leaving shortly but you will be permitted to take your father's carriage into London, then spend the night at my house under my charge.'

This was wonderful news indeed. Spending the night at his residence. Could it possibly get any better?

'I think you should thank your father now for his generous gesture of trust and goodwill.'

'Yes, sir, of course,' she replied, and skipped past him as he ushered her out the door. 'I shall do so immediately.'

When Lord Michael left that afternoon, Elizabeth was so thrilled at the prospect of the following evening every ounce of her earlier depression had evaporated. She would spend the rest of the day deciding which clothes to wear and what to pack, and have Grace play with her hair until a style worthy of the occasion could be decided upon.

She did so admire him, she thought, watching the carriage he was in disappear down the drive. She waited until he was completely out of sight, and then went back indoors, her brother beside her.

'So, he's quite a chap, isn't he, Elizabeth?' her sibling said.

'Yes, James, he certainly is,' she concurred.

'You need a strong male partner like him,' he went on, unwittingly echoing her very thoughts. 'The usual type that simper around you are no good at all.'

The old Elizabeth would have turned on him and told him off, insisting he mind his own business, and if she chose to spend time with those 'simpering' others, then she would.

But the new Elizabeth nodded agreeably, and turning to look at her brother, agreed utterly. 'Oh, James,' she said with an intensity that surprised even her, 'you're so right. To think I might have wasted myself on any one of them!'

James almost hugged her. He would certainly shake Lord Michael's hand when next they saw each other, for in a matter of mere days in his company his sister had turned into a good-natured, well-mannered, very pleasant young lady.

'Would you excuse me, dear James?' she said, completely unable to contain herself. 'But I'm so thrilled about tomorrow night I simply must start preparing myself now.'

Still stunned by this remarkable turnaround, he did not quite know how to respond to such a polite and fervent request, and was even more shocked when she didn't dash off, but stood politely awaiting his response.

'Do you mind?' she prompted.

'Elizabeth, it is such a delight to see you this way,' he said. 'Of course you may go, and if there's anything I can do to help, just let me know.'

She smiled and thanked him, then disappeared up the

stairs. James, still disbelieving, made his way to the study.

'She's a different girl, father,' he said, as he sat in one of the large leather armchairs.

His father raised his head from the newspaper and nodded. 'She is indeed. I can only hope my good friend will continue in his affections, and perhaps even one of these days make an honest woman of her.'

'I hope so too,' James agreed. 'For all our sakes, I hope so too.'

Up in her room Elizabeth was going through her dresses. She wasn't happy with any of them, and over the course of the evening, interrupted by a very quick dinner, chose four, discarded those, and finally settled on a royal blue silk that highlighted her skin tones, and brought out the colour of her eyes.

With Grace's help she also decided upon a hairstyle, and by the time she had bathed and was climbing into bed, she was exhausted.

In the darkness she wriggled under the covers. She missed him. She missed the stinging of her bottom, of him making love to her, of curling up next to him, totally spent, feeling safe and warm, but most of all, she missed being under his complete control.

She was being such a good girl, learning to follow his orders immediately and without question. But then she furrowed her brow, for this being the case, would she never again feel the painfully exquisite sting of his discipline?

And why did she crave such excruciating attention? But even as she asked the question, she knew she may never know the answer. She just did; she craved to be punished, made to behave, then taken and driven to the heights of passion. Was there anything better in the whole world?

The questions flittered through her mind. The only answer, she decided, was to purposely misbehave, so he would have no choice but to continue keeping her within the bounds of acceptable behaviour by the use of corporal punishment.

The thought made her tremble a little; the memory of how the hairbrush stung her cheeks and how the crop bit into her flesh made her shudder. Did she really want this? She touched between her legs, feeling the wetness there. Yes she did. The memories of his discipline spurred her on until the moment was upon her, and she released her joy with small cries of pleasure.

It was the first time she had experienced an orgasm without him. The first time, alone in the dark, she had found her own satisfaction. It wasn't the same, but it helped, and she was finally able to sleep.

When she awoke the following morning she did so determined to find a way to misbehave at dinner. It was the only thing she could think of to ensure a trip across his knee, or over the sofa, or tied over a pillow. Just the thought made her positively tingle, and pleased with herself, she made her way to the bathroom to ready herself for the day, and the exciting evening that lay ahead.

Chapter Eleven

Lord Michael watched Elizabeth intently as she eyed the decadent dessert. They were seated in the dining room of an elegant London hotel, the admiring glances being cast their way pleasing them both.

It was clear she was still in need of much training. Her spoiled past and wilful nature could not be completely corrected in such a short space of time. Though he had to admit she had behaved admirably when they arrived back at the manor, and so far this evening he had nothing about which he could complain or correct her for.

He recalled the many times he had observed her over the past few years, and how frequently in that time he wished he could put her over his knee. His dear friend, her father, had been absolutely correct when he said she was a handful, but he knew he was more than up to the task, and she was responding exactly as he had hoped and judged she would. Besides which, despite her tender years compared to his he had to admit the little minx was under his skin. Since leaving her the day before he had thought of her constantly.

She knew she was not permitted to eat until he signalled her to do so. It was her favourite desert, hot apple pie and cream, and it seemed an age since the steaming dish had been placed in front of her. She looked at him, the previous expression of innocent pleading replaced by coolly controlled frustration.

This was her opportunity, she thought to herself. This

was the perfect chance to misbehave. So heart pounding, she said, 'How long do you intend to keep me from eating my dessert?' Her tone had a petulant edge to it that she knew would rankle with him, and she was meeting his stare with a challenge in her eyes. For a moment she thought he was on the back foot, but she should have known better.

He placed his coffee cup on its saucer with a dangerous, calculated precision, his eyes never leaving hers. 'Have you completely lost your mind, Elizabeth?' he asked coldly, noting with relish the flicker of uncertainty in her lovely face. 'Have you completely forgotten your place when in my company?'

'I…' her confidence quickly ebbed, 'I… it's just that…' Perhaps her little game was ill advised after all, she thought, attempting to convey a sense of self-assurance she was suddenly no longer feeling.

Lord Michael studied her. Something was amiss. She knew better than to test him this way. He furrowed his brow and cocked his head to one side.

The silence and gesture made Elizabeth decidedly nervous. Why wasn't he saying anything? Surely he would have to spank her for such a childish outburst? But he did nothing, simply remained silent, frowning at her.

Feeling she'd already gone too far and could not turn back, that she had little choice but to force the issue, she compounded the situation by blurting, 'My apple pie is getting cold and it will soon be ruined, so I will commence eating now anyway, with or without your consent,' and so saying she picked up her dessert spoon and fork.

'I don't believe you, young lady,' he said, his words instantly halting the movement of her cutlery.

'W-what do you mean?' she gasped.

'I mean, you know better than to behave this way, so I don't believe you. I think there's more to this little scene. I don't believe you're worried about your dessert spoiling at all.'

The rising flush in her cheeks told him he was right, of course. She was attempting to manipulate him. She had fallen in love with the ritual of punishment, with the joys a sound spanking could offer, and she wanted to instigate one. And rather than ask or convey her feelings and yearnings, she had all too easily returned to her old habits, using manipulation and contrivance to get her own way.

Without a word Lord Michael opened his wallet, withdrew the notes needed to cover the bill, then rose majestically and with purpose. Elizabeth, knowing she'd lost control and that her mischievousness had not been appreciated whatsoever, felt the recently arrived flush drain from her face. Although a spanking or chastisement of some sort had been her goal, she knew she had overstepped some sort of marker and the mood between them was not what she'd planned or wanted.

He took her by the forearm, his fierce grip making her wince, and pulled her ungracefully from her chair. She attempted to speak, to gush a discreet protest, but he shot her a look so stern the words never even reached her lips. Well at least she was to be punished, she thought ruefully as a member of the restaurant staff brought their coats, but then she shivered, worried about the severity of what was to come, worried that she'd overdone her little ploy.

He maintained his unnerving silence on the carriage ride home, and when they pulled up outside his house he turned and addressed her. 'Elizabeth, I am utterly disappointed in you,' he said, his few words cutting her to the core.

'After all my attention, after all the time and effort I have invested in your education, this is how you repay me?'

Elizabeth felt the tears well up in her eyes, panic rising from her stomach until she felt quite queasy with despair. 'But, sir—'

'Be quiet!' he snapped. 'I do not wish to hear anything you have to say or any of your feeble platitudes. Your pathetic attempt to manipulate me is hurtful indeed. Do you think I am one of those foolish young lads that you manoeuvre to get your own spoilt way? You wanted to be spanked, to be firmly taken in hand, and rather than confess your longings you tried to trick me. Shame on you, Elizabeth. Shame on you.'

Shimmering tears began to spill down her face. 'Sir, I'm so very sorry,' she wailed. 'How can I make it up to you?'

'You cannot,' he stated adamantly. 'You wanted to be punished? Well, now you will be. You will receive the ultimate punishment; I shall have nothing more to do with you.'

Elizabeth's expression froze as his cruel words hit her.

'To think I was seriously considering becoming your master,' he added.

'Oh please, sir,' she begged desperately, her head in a spin, trying not to accept the reality of what he was saying, cursing her earlier folly. 'Please, I beg you to reconsider. I am a foolish girl, still learning from you. Oh please, I do so want to serve you. I beg you, please give me another chance!'

He glared back at her, unmoved by her hysteria. 'Tonight you will be staying here at my house,' he told her. 'Nancy, my housemaid, will see to your needs, and you will return to your home tomorrow. I, however, will

149

spend the night at my club. This is goodbye, Elizabeth. Certainly for the foreseeable future.'

'But…'

Before she could say any more he climbed determinedly from the carriage and strode quickly away into the night. Elizabeth collapsed in desperate tears. How foolish she had been. How could she have been so stupid as to think she could play games with one such as he and get away with it? She could not stop sobbing, but finally realised she should get out of the carriage and inside the house.

The housemaid answered her timid knock, and when she saw the tragic state the poor girl was in, immediately dropped any formality and put a comforting arm around her shoulders. She offered to make her a hot cup of tea, but Elizabeth was inconsolable. Regardless, she brewed one, and brought it into the sitting room where Elizabeth was sitting on the couch, still in her coat, still crying.

'Miss Elizabeth, I know Lord Michael can be strict, but surely whatever's happened he'll forgive you.'

Elizabeth shook her head. 'I don't think so,' she managed between sobs. 'He said he wants nothing more to do with me.'

'He probably just spoke out of anger,' Nancy said, trying to reassure her. 'Can you tell me what happened? Perhaps I can help.'

Elizabeth shook her head adamantly. How could she possibly explain such a thing to anyone, let alone someone she didn't know, and a servant at that?

'Give it some time,' the pretty housemaid suggested. 'Men are forgiving creatures, and I know he thinks a great deal of you.'

'He does?' Elizabeth looked up at the girl, boosted by a faint ray of hope. 'How do you know that?'

'He told me a little about you,' Nancy confided, 'when he informed me there'd be a guest staying tonight. It was obvious he was looking forward to your stay here immensely.'

Elizabeth put her handkerchief to her face and dabbed at the tears, and Nancy took the break in the weeping to remove Elizabeth's coat and offer her the cup of tea. Elizabeth drank it gratefully, fixating on Nancy's last remark.

'When you leave tomorrow, do so believing it will only be a matter of time before he misses you and sends word,' the housemaid told her, and Elizabeth nodded, suppressed the new wave of tears that threatened, and managed to finish the revitalising cup of tea.

'Thank you, she said,' passing the cup and saucer back and managing a smile of appreciation. 'You're so kind. A beast like *him* doesn't deserve you,' she added spitefully, not really meaning it.

'Well, I've been with Lord Michael for many years,' the servant informed her. 'Since I was thirteen, in fact, when my mother came into service for him. He's been very good to us. He made sure I learned how to read and write and taught me a great deal. I could do other things, but I'm happy here.'

'Yes,' Elizabeth said, nodding. She could imagine Lord Michael doing such a thing, giving a girl the opportunity to better herself.

Nancy accompanied her up to the guest bedroom, and Elizabeth could not help but think had she not been so impetuously guileless, so bound to have her way, that she would have been spending the night in his room, in his bed, in his arms.

Once under the covers of the comfortable bed Elizabeth

cried some more, then tried to sleep. She tossed and turned, and prayed and hoped, and in the early hours of the morning, overcome by tiredness, she eventually drifted into a fitful sleep.

When Nancy woke her the following morning Elizabeth felt as though she'd been thrown from her horse. Her body ached, her head ached, and when she looked in the mirror the eyes that stared back at her were puffy and red, with dark bags beneath them. She looked as miserable as she felt.

She attempted to eat the breakfast prepared for her, but she had no appetite and merely picked at it for a while with her fork. She drank half a cup of tea, then thanked Nancy and headed home, the carriage ride back to the manor seeming long and lonely, and the tears kept threatening.

When close to home she attempted to compose herself, not wanting anyone to see what a state she was in. She certainly would not be able to explain herself. What could she possibly say? But when she arrived home she was grateful that her brother was nowhere to be seen, and her father was working in his study.

She hastened up to her room, and once inside locked the door. Then she collapsed on her bed and cried a fresh flood of tears, but a knock on the door forced her to stop crying and try to gather her composure. She heard Grace's voice.

'I'm resting,' she called. 'I won't be down for dinner. I'm tired. Tell father, and don't bother me again until morning.'

Sitting up she wiped her face and made her way to the bathroom. She decided to fill the bath, sprinkling in some rose scent. It reminded her of the last time she'd done just that. How alarmed she had been, and then strangely stirred, when he'd touched her so intimately that night…

A new set of tears threatened, but with a deep breath she willed them away. Stripping off her clothes she stepped into the steamy water and sank down. The soothing heat and fragrance really helped, and she closed her eyes, recalling his face. Despite his age she was in love with him, she decided. Totally and unequivocally, and more than anything else she wanted to serve him. She wanted to call him her master.

She opened her eyes, a sense of purpose welling up inside her. She would not lose him, no matter what. She didn't know how but she would win him back, and by the time she stepped from the bath with a new determination and resolve she felt much, much better. She would regroup, and then take some definite, honest, and forthright action.

Lord Michael was back at his house. He was not just angry with Elizabeth, but grossly disappointed. Up until that point he was sure she would prove to be a more than worthy and long-term student, but one thing he would not tolerate was deceit. How could he possibly trust her after she'd played such a silly game on him? She had belittled everything he'd taught her and in doing so insulted him utterly.

All afternoon he paced in his study, important papers lying unattended on his desk. Try as he might he could not get her out of his mind. Then late in the day Nancy appeared, carrying a tray of tea and scones. Carefully she set it on the side table and then turned to face him. His mood was dark.

'Sir?' she began, hesitantly.

'Yes?' he responded absently, not looking at her.

'I just thought you should know, sir,' the maid ventured carefully, 'that she was inconsolable, and I know she cried throughout the night. Whatever her crime, she is truly repentant.'

Lord Michael looked at her. It was not her place to speak of things so personal, but she had been under his discipline for most of her life, and he knew she would not do or say anything unless she felt it to be for the best.

'Thank you, Nancy,' he said. 'That will be all.'

Knowing she could say no more she curtsied and left, hoping she'd done the right thing.

Lord Michael poured himself some tea and sat down. He pondered Nancy's words. He had to admit, he did want to forgive Elizabeth... the naughty, brazen girl!

In his mind's eye he saw her delightful smile, and suddenly wanted to smell her hair, to touch her skin. The truth was he wanted to guide her through the many layers and peaks and troughs of submission. He wanted to be her master.

The epiphany shook him. Yes, he'd been considering it, but until that moment he had not realised what a truism it was. What he would do about it he did not know, but the revelation made him feel much better and settled.

He decided then that he would let her suffer for a few days more, allow the pain of his absence to be a part of her punishment. It was certainly no less than she deserved. Then once he'd given the matter more thought in his own time, he would decide upon a suitable course of action.

Chapter Twelve

After five days with no word from Lord Michael, Elizabeth decided it was time to take matters in hand. She missed him terribly, so no matter what her punishment, no matter what she would have to endure, she wanted to pay the price for her mistake and hoped he might then forgive her. She had learned her lesson, and if given a second chance she would never play childish games or try to manipulate him again.

She had two choices. She could write him a heartfelt apology, begging his forgiveness, or she could go to him and throw herself at his feet. Besides the fact that writing was not really her style, she longed to see him. But would he even listen to her, let alone see her?

Taking a deep breath of resolve she cast aside her doubts. She wanted to put her case in person. She at least had to try that, and if he was not receptive, well, so then she would at least know where she stood, so she ran to her father's study and knocked on the door, it not even occurring to her that only a short while before she would have burst in uninvited. In a short space of time Lord Michael had taught her well. She heard her father's voice permitting entry, and entered.

'Hello, my dear,' he said. 'I've not seen much of you this week. Are you quite well? You're not feeling under the weather, are you?'

'No, father, I'm fine,' she insisted, but I've urgent business with Lord Michael and I wondered if I might take the carriage? Or even the little cab?'

Her father studied her for a few moments. He had known something was amiss. She'd barely said two sentences to him since her evening in London, and she'd looked quite miserable on the few occasions he had been in her company.

'Before I allow you to go, you must tell me what's happened,' he said, not sure whether to expect a sharp retort from the old Elizabeth, or an honest explanation from the seemingly reformed version.

'Oh, father,' she sighed, 'I'm afraid I've made a frightful mess of things. I've foolishly toyed with Lord Michael,' she said, choosing her words carefully, 'and of course he realised it right away. It was silly and thoughtless and ill mannered of me, and I just want to see if I can make things right again between us. I have to try, at least. I cannot bear him thinking ill of me, or thinking me an immature girl.'

Her father could see she was completely sincere, and there was nothing more he wanted than to see his daughter happily married to a fine gentleman like his good friend. For one thing, it was clear he knew how to handle the difficult girl, and regardless of how fond he was of his daughter, she could be downright incorrigible. 'Of course you must go, my dear,' he said warmly. 'I'll not be requiring the carriage for a while, so go to town in that. If you leave now you'll arrive in time for lunch. Perhaps sharing a nice meal might help the conversation.'

'Father, thank you!' she cried, and gave him a huge hug and kissed him on the cheek with such an instinctive display of exuberant affection that he was left chuckling and bumbling.

'I hope he forgives you,' he blustered cheerfully. 'Really

I do.'

Elizabeth ran to her room, changed quickly, and throwing just the essentials and some money in her bag, she headed off to arrange her transport.

In London Lord Michael was readying himself for an important business luncheon. He'd decided to travel to the country over the coming weekend, to visit the inveterate Elizabeth and have a particularly stern talk with her to determine whether or not she had seen the significant error of her ways. Having made up his mind, he was now able to concentrate on the matter at hand. The business venture he was meeting about was the same one he'd been studying when Elizabeth had disobediently ridden off into the storm, and the memory of her stubborn insubordination made him smile.

He felt himself stir at the memory. How fearful he'd been that she would be harmed, or fall seriously ill. Then his mind wandered to her punishment, and he shook his head ruefully; such a recalcitrant young woman, but so beautifully spirited with it.

He broke from his reverie and returned to his work, and began making notes for the meeting's agenda. He worked through the morning, stopping only for a cup of coffee, as was his habit, at eleven. Eventually the ornate clock on the mantelpiece chimed noon, signalling it was time for him to leave. The meeting over luncheon was scheduled for one o'clock, at his club.

As he gathered his paperwork and sorted it into his briefcase, he heard a knock at the front door, but paid it no heed; Nancy would take care of it. So he took his jacked from the peg on the study door and slipped into it, giving it a quick brush down with his palm.

Just as he put his hand on the door handle to leave the study there was a knock from the other side, so he opened it anyway to see Nancy standing in the hall, her knuckle poised in mid-air in case there was the need to knock again. She was taken a little by surprise, not expecting the door to open so instantly.

'What is it, Nancy?' he asked.

'I think you should come and see for yourself, sir,' she said cryptically. 'You have an unexpected visitor.'

Frowning and impatiently checking the time again, on this occasion from the timepiece in his fob, Lord Michael made his way to the sitting room, and standing by the fireplace, nervously fidgeting with her purse, was Elizabeth.

He could not believe his eyes. The brazen girl had travelled all the way to London and entered his house without being invited! But on the other hand, he had to confess she looked quite beautiful, as usual. Her face was flushed, her eyes sparkling, and her shapely figure was deftly outlined by her exquisite dress, and despite being dumbfounded by her temerity, his penis stirred immediately.

'Elizabeth,' he said, emphasising an air of indifference, even annoyance, 'what is the meaning of this?' He heard Nancy quietly close the door behind him, tactfully knowing when it was time to retreat and leave her employer to deal with issues at hand.

'My lord,' she began, having inhaled deeply to summon her courage, the gentleman before her unable to miss the delightful swell of her breasts within her dress as she did so, 'I am a foolish, spoiled, misbehaved young chit of a girl. Everything you said of me last week was true. I cannot undo what I did. All I can do is tell you that I'm most dreadfully sorry, and I will never, ever play games with you again, and I have come here to ask your forgiveness.

'I miss you, sir,' she went on stoutly, her courage restored, 'but I only want to please you, and so if my apology is not acceptable I shall leave you now and you will not be bothered again by an emotional triviality like me. That is all I want to say, sir.'

The gentleman was moved by her sincerity, and by her courageous determination in making such an effort to travel alone to London to confront him in person. He admired her for it immensely, and it would also appear she had learned her lesson.

'I see,' he responded coolly, giving nothing away. 'Well, you have caught me at an inconvenient time, and that's a fact. I have a very important luncheon meeting to attend. I shall consider what you have had to say for yourself and respond in a manner appropriate at a time of my choosing.'

Elizabeth's heart jumped with hope; he hadn't sent her on her way and was apparently prepared to see her again later.

'I should warn you, however,' he went on, 'that if I were to forgive you there will be a penalty to pay for the way you behaved.'

Her face flushed and she stared meekly at the floor.

'I shall leave you with this thought,' he summed up. 'You attempted to manipulate me in order to have me tan your bottom. Isn't that right?'

'Yes, sir,' she admitted, embarrassed and ashamed.

'So if I decide to forgive you, you shall indeed get what you wanted. However, I can assure you there will be nothing pleasurable about it. Consider that, and you have my permission to alter your thinking or review your position having spent the afternoon doing so. If you are not here when I return, I will not be surprised.'

'I'll be here, sir,' she answered quickly and determinedly.

'We'll see,' he said doubtfully. 'And now I must go. By turning up on my doorstep unannounced you have put me in danger of being late for my very important meeting.'

'Yes sir,' she blurted, 'sorry sir.'

She remained standing until she heard the front door close behind him, then dropped down onto the sofa, the tension of the brief meeting and the long battle of resolve leading up to it suddenly making her feel exhausted. During the journey to London she had practiced her speech repeatedly, and she had been so nervous as she delivered it she could barely breathe. Now he was gone she felt quite weak.

The door opened a fraction and Nancy peeped in. 'Forgive me for asking, miss,' she said hesitantly, 'but are you forgiven?'

'I don't know,' Elizabeth replied honestly, grateful to have someone to confide in, despite it being a servant. 'He said he'd tell me when he has more time and it suits him to do so.'

'I see,' said Nancy, nodding as though she knew exactly what that meant. 'In the meantime, would you care for some lunch, miss?' she went on brightly.

'Oh dear,' Elizabeth replied, 'I fear I'm far too on edge to eat.'

'But you should try to have a little something, at least,' the maid tried again. 'You need to keep your strength up. You'll only make yourself ill, otherwise.'

Elizabeth knew she was right, and so she smiled appreciatively and accepted the offer.

It was not difficult for Lord Michael to concentrate on his meeting. Elizabeth's unannounced arrival had put his mind at rest on certain matters. She was back in his life, and the fact that she'd taken such an initiative spoke well of her strength of character. There was no doubt she wanted to submit to him, to learn all he had to teach her, and she would start by paying dearly for her infraction. Of that there was no doubt.

Having eaten with his business associate and concluded their meeting, he spent the rest of the afternoon at his club, and when he finally returned home he did so with a pleasurable knot of expectation in his stomach. It promised to be a very interesting evening.

Elizabeth had spent the afternoon and early evening full of apprehension and uncertainty. She had managed a sandwich and a cup of tea, but could not face anything more than that. By the time the dinner approached she was truly hungry, but her stomach was tied up in knots.

She took care as she dressed, wanting to look as pretty as she could, and when she entered the dining room she was surprised to find Lord Michael waiting for her. She hadn't heard him come home.

'Elizabeth,' he said, greeting her, but he did not approach her or reach for her hand.

'Good evening, sir,' she replied politely.

'Please sit,' he said, gesturing at the table. 'I believe the cook has prepared something quite delicious for us.'

A maid entered carrying a casserole of some kind, and followed it with boiled potatoes and carrots.

'Ah yes,' he said, inhaling the mouth-watering smells coming from the large dish, 'it is indeed her famous stew. I never know what's in it, but it is delicious beyond compare.'

The girl served them and left, and remembering her training Elizabeth sat quietly, the plate of steaming and tasty-looking food before her.

Lord Michael looked at her. 'Why aren't you eating, Elizabeth?' he asked.

'Because you've not yet given me permission to begin,' she replied.

'But you're no longer under my influence,' he pointed out, being intentionally blunt, as though he cared not a jot whether she was or whether she wasn't.

Elizabeth took a sip of her red wine, hoping to suppress her feelings of defeatism, and then she picked up her knife and fork. Lord Michael knew the words and his indifferent manner had hit home, for she looked decidedly despondent, but he needed her to understand her previous behaviour was not a small matter. It was necessary for her to believe the situation was irretrievable, and he sensed that was already very nearly, if not completely, what she did believe.

'Sir,' she suddenly said, having eaten a particularly succulent piece of beef that warmed her tummy and instantly made her feel better and more at ease, 'I would ask you not to keep me in suspense any longer. If you wish to banish me from your home and your company, then please do so now. I cannot stand this uncertainty and tension another moment. Truly I can't. If there remains irreparable ill-feeling between us it is better that I leave.'

'Hmm, I seem to remember patience being one of the most difficult qualities to teach you,' he said, rising from his chair. She watched him approach her and felt her pulse quicken, and when he reached out a hand she accepted it and he led her to the small settee by the window. He sat down and indicated she was to kneel in front of him. 'So, you want to know where we stand, do you?' he asked.

'If it pleases you, sir, I do, yes,' she said, remembering the respectful phraseology he'd taught her.

'I see.' He thought for a while, gazing out of the window. 'And have you considered what I told you earlier? If I decide to forgive you, you will extract no pleasure from your punishment. It certainly will not be what you've been seeking or what you felt you've been missing.'

Elizabeth shivered, and steeled herself to go on. 'I... I have considered what you said, sir, but fleetingly,' she told him. 'For there is very little I would not endure to be back in your good graces, subject to your discipline and authority.'

He was glad she had said 'very little' as opposed to 'nothing'. It was a small distinction but an important one, for it showed that despite the training she had undergone thus far she still had her pride, spirit, and character intact – and he would not wish to strip her utterly of those.

'Let me warn you now, Elizabeth, that if you ever again treat me or the training regime I put you through lightly, if you ever attempt to cheek me or manipulate my good nature in any way at all, no matter how small, you will be banished from my company and there will be no more reprieves. Do you understand me clearly, young lady? I will not be repeating myself on this matter.'

'Yes, sir,' she said contritely, his words really sinking in, 'that is perfectly clear. Never, ever again, sir, I can assure you of that, no matter what.'

He considered the openness of her face, and in particular her eyes, a little while longer, then made his mind up. 'Very well,' he decided, 'your sincerity has moved me and convinced me, and I believe you are truly repentant.'

'Oh I am, sir!' she beamed, the weight of the world suddenly seeming to lift from her slender shoulders. 'I am filled with remorse and regret,' she assured him.

'All right, Elizabeth, all right,' he said, raising a palm to forestall any further outpourings of contrition. 'I believe you.'

'Oh sir!' she beamed, kissing his hands.

'But I am going to sentence you now, Elizabeth,' he said ominously. 'Pay attention, and realise what it is you will be agreeing to.'

'Yes, sir,' she said, looking up at him with earnest hope in her eyes, 'I'm listening carefully.'

'You shall receive six strokes of the cane,' he announced. 'I know you have not experienced the bite of the cane yet. I reserve it for only the harshest punishments, never to be forgotten.'

Elizabeth felt her haunches tense. She was aware of the dreaded rod, and now she was to experience its venomous sting for real. A shiver ran up her spine.

'Shall I continue, Elizabeth?' he tested her. 'Do you accept the cane?'

'I… um… y-yes, sir,' she answered uncertainly.

'Very well,' he said solemnly. 'Thereafter you will be brought to the point of orgasm but not allowed release three times a day, for four days. Do you accept this stage of the punishment, Elizabeth?'

'Yes, sir,' she answered, wondering how she would be able to endure, but willing to try. 'But if I am to stay here with you I must inform my father—'

'I will take care of all such matters.' He waited to ensure there were to be no further outbursts concerning the more practical logistics of her punishment.

'You will sleep on the floor next to my bed,' he continued, after a long enough pause assured him she was finished. 'You will have a pillow and blanket, but that is all. Do you accept this?'

'Yes, sir, if it is to be, then I do accept it.'

'And lastly, you will receive no affection from me whatsoever. Apart from the necessary minimum requirement to expedite your punishment, I will pay you little attention, and will speak to you only when I absolutely have to. And you will not speak to me unless spoken to, and you will not be permitted to leave the house during the length of your sentence. Is that all completely understood, young lady?'

At least she would be with him. 'Yes, sir,' she said quietly.

'Very good, that is settled, then,' he decreed. 'In the morning I shall send word to your father. I am sure he will be most agreeable to my plans. Now take yourself up to my bedroom, remove all your clothes and bend over the foot of my bed and wait.'

He watched her leave obediently without another word, and then returned to his tasty dinner. He ate heartily, and thought how pretty her bottom would look marked with the strokes of his cane. He finished his wine, ate a little fruit and cream, then made his way up to his room.

Elizabeth, bent across the foot of the bed as she'd been told to, was filled with trepidation and fear. She wondered just how bad it would be, and when she heard the door opening she squirmed anxiously.

She waited to feel his hand caress her taut flesh, as was his usual manner, but he didn't. Then she remembered his edict. There was to be no affection and minimal touching. Then suddenly she yelped as he grabbed her hair and abruptly pulled her up straight. He placed a blindfold of unyieldingly heavy leather across her eyes, and there was nothing sensuous or comforting about it.

'Open your mouth,' he ordered curtly.

She did so, and he gagged her with a musty piece of cloth.

'Wrists.'

She blindly offered them to him, lifting them before her. He bound them together then pulled her forward. She fell across the bed and immediately felt his hands at her ankles, tying them together with some sort of rope.

She then heard him moving around the room, the opening and closing of a wardrobe door, then the dreaded cane was resting on the silky smooth slopes of her vulnerable bottom.

He held it there for long breathless moments, admiring the vision before him. Her porcelain-white moons were delectable indeed... *she* was delectable indeed.

There was no escape for her now. He'd outlined the punishment and she'd accepted it, and now the first stage was to be carried out. He slid the cane back and forth across her skin, concentrating on his target, adding to her apprehension, and then raising the whippy implement meaningfully he paused again, hand high above his head, then swept his arm down with the full weight of his shoulder behind it. The cane hissed through air, landing across her flesh with a cruel *crack!*

The gorgeous girl stiffened, as though unable to believe the pain or import of what he'd just inflicted upon her, and had the air not caught in her lungs she would have screamed the house down. As it was her mouth gaped and she chewed the gag, but no coherent sound emerged from her tensed body. Instantly a bright red stripe rose and dissected her bottom from one buttock to the other, spanning the deep and shadowy divide.

He rested the tip of the rod on the small of her back,

leaving it there, then leaned forward.

'Stroke number one,' he whispered callously.

A branding iron could not have been worse, searing her flesh. She felt the tears trying to squeeze from the corners of her tightly clamped eyelids, but strained to fight them back, not wanting to admit to herself or to him that the very first single strike had almost broken her. She was panting through the gag. The burning in her bottom wasn't easing, and she still had five strokes to go. Feeling the rod resting on her lower back, she wondered how long she would be made to wait before the next appalling stroke was applied.

Then she realised something was tickling her clitoris. It didn't feel like a finger, but whatever it was, it was insistent, sliding back and forth, circling her most sensitive button. She could not help but writhe a little, at least as much as her bonds would allow. Whatever it was rubbed more aggressively and she felt herself growing wet from its attention. It was insistent, toying and playing between her sex lips, and she moaned into the gag with pleasure. She wondered if she'd misunderstood him, because she could already feel a bubble of bliss beginning to grow. Just a minute or two more of such delightful teasing…

She felt the rod being moved from her back, and it settled a couple of inches below the throbbing mark of the first stroke. Lord Michael heard her take a deep breath, then lifting it he paused ritually, eyed the delicious target below, then swept his arm down with equally vehement velocity as he used for the first strike. The cane sank into her flesh with savage force and she jerked her head up, writhing in torment, squealing through the gag.

'Stroke number two,' he declared precisely, watching her squirm, the cheeks of her bottom gyrating unintentionally salaciously.

'Should I stop now, Elizabeth?' he goaded. 'You can always save yourself such punishment and go home; return to your former life.'

Despite being very nearly tempted to do just that, she shook her head fervently, determined to overcome.

'I did warn you,' he continued. 'There is no pleasure in this, is there, my dear?' Again she shook her head. 'You wanted your bottom warmed, so perhaps this will teach you to be careful what you ask for.'

Resting the cane on the small of her back once more, he moved the riding crop and began to tease her again, and very soon heard the telltale panting of arousal and removed it, then smiling with satisfaction at the two wicked welts he'd adorned her exquisite rump with, he moved silently away and left the room.

Elizabeth barely heard the door open and close, but she was aware of it. She was beside herself with desire, but the scorching pain in her buttocks compounded this. She was paying dearly for her misbehaviour, and he was right; she would never, ever forget this. At that moment she hoped she would never again give him cause to cane her so stringently.

The minutes ticked slowly by, and Elizabeth had no idea how much time was passing. The lull seemed endless, she was beginning to ache from being in one position for so long, and her stinging welts were no less keen.

When she heard the door open again she breathed a sigh of relief, but it was momentary. Without a word the rod was lifted off her back, and seconds later it landed across the middle of her tensed rear, wrenching an unbidden muffled shriek from her lungs.

'Stroke number three,' he proclaimed, and before she

had time to engage her thoughts it landed once more, blistering her skin with a line of fire. She shrieked again, and despite her best efforts the tears started to squeeze from beneath the blindfold.

'Stroke number four.'

He slid the rod between her thighs, skimming it between her sex lips, and despite the scalding anguish of her bottom she could not help but surrender to the erotic torment. She wriggled, and Lord Michael enjoyed the view of her movements and her striped bottom as she tried to pleasure herself against the teasing stick. But it was to no avail. As soon as her panting sighs revealed the state of her arousal he returned it to its resting place, where it forewarned of its potency, across her lower back.

Nancy entered silently, carrying a blanket and pillow, casting a glance at the victim's punished behind. She knew how she felt, for once upon a time, not so long ago, she'd suffered the same sentence. And even now, on the first day of every month, she would lift her skirt, bend over the back of the sofa in the sitting room, and Lord Michael would give her a single powerful stroke. It was all she needed to remain submissive and compliant, and the truth was there were times when she looked forward to it immensely, for it helped her maintain an emotional balance.

She laid the pillow and blanket on the floor next to her master's bed, and with a curtsy, left and closed the door. Elizabeth had been completely unaware of her brief presence.

He began to prepare for bed. He went to the adjoining bathroom and ran a bath, then disrobed, folding his clothes neatly and placing them in the hamper. He took his time, and when the bath was full he returned to finish the caning.

He picked up the rod, and without a word or fuss he

laid it against the lower curve of Elizabeth's bottom. He raised it, swept it down again, and listened to the now familiar muffled shriek.

'Stroke number five,' he said uncompromisingly, wondering if he should lay on the last cut immediately or wait until after his bath. He decided to finish the job, untie her, and order her to her place on the floor. He could then go directly to bed after bathing.

So having decided he raised the rod again and cut it swiftly down across the milky cheeks, savouring the delicious sight of them quivering as the wooden implement sank into their softness. He knew very well the beaten area would now be acutely sensitive, and the stroke would smart immeasurably more than those that visited her rear previously, but that did not cause him to ease up on her. She deserved all she received, and no mistake.

'Stroke number six,' he said as she howled into the gag, her toes curling and her fingers clutching at thin air, and then he returned the rod to its cabinet.

He returned to her, viewed his handiwork proudly, and then waited until she appeared sufficiently composed. He removed the blindfold and the gag, and untied her ankles and wrists. Then helping her to the blanket and pillow he ordered her to bed, and then took his bath. He could hear her moaning softly throughout, and was satisfied that the girl had been soundly caned.

As Elizabeth lay under the rough blanket she ached for his comforting arms. Her bottom was scalded and throbbing horribly, and she had no idea how much she would miss his affection after such a punishment, but it was all part of her sentence. She had to pay the price to prove her commitment and remorse, and she was a very sorry girl indeed.

170

By the time he emerged from the bathroom Elizabeth felt a deal calmer, though the intense burning had barely eased at all. He climbed into bed, and as he doused the bedside lamp he gave her one last instruction.

'No touching yourself, Elizabeth,' he said. 'You may comfort your sore bottom if you need to, and if you can bear to touch it, but you are not to relieve any sexual frustrations in any way. Do you understand me?'

'Yes, sir,' she said weakly, her voice a whisper.

The following morning Elizabeth was woken sharply by the blanket being pulled from her aching body. He was standing over her, fully dressed, ready for the day, holding a tapered crop. He tapped the insides of her thighs, forcing them apart, and then placed the tip of the leather implement directly against her clitoris.

She was startled and still half asleep, but that didn't stop her body from responding. He probed and toyed and soon she was squirming, wanting more. It was a cruel instrument indeed, and with his skill it was enough to drive her mad with lust, but deliberately not to the point of taking her over the brink.

How long he tortured her she did not know, but eventually he ordered her to her feet, and she stood unsteadily. He reached between her legs, and satisfied with her wetness, he heartlessly turned and left the room.

She was burning with need and she was craving release. Her bottom was tender and sore, but she did not have time to give it any real thought, for the door opened and Nancy appeared, carrying towels and some fresh clothes.

Suddenly embarrassed at her nakedness, Elizabeth snatched up the blanket and attempted to cover herself, but her state of undress did not seem to bother Nancy at all. She barely glanced in her direction, going straight to the bathroom to run a bath.

Still clutching the blanket Elizabeth tentatively moved to the open doorway, and Nancy looked up and smiled at her.

'It appears you've been forgiven,' she said cheerfully.

'Um, yes,' Elizabeth concurred, a little unsure of herself, 'it would appear so.'

'Your punishment will be over before you know it,' the housemaid opined. 'Lord Michael has sent for some of your things, but in the meantime here are some fresh clothes.'

'Thank you,' she said gratefully, a little surprised by the familiarity the maid was still showing her. It was a very different situation than that to which she was accustomed.

'When you're dressed you are to come downstairs,' the maid informed her. 'There'll be some breakfast waiting for you in the dining room, and you may then do as you please for the rest of the morning, although Lord Michael has said you will report to him in his study at one o'clock.'

Then glancing at the bathwater she added, 'I'll leave you to it now.' She gave Elizabeth another smile, and then left her alone.

Elizabeth folded the blanket and placed it next to the pillow, then went back to the bathroom. Lowering herself into the hot water she winced as it lapped her ravaged bottom, but gradually the severe sensations eased and submersed herself up to her shoulders, lying back and relaxing in its revitalising heat.

As she picked up the soap and began to wash, she knew she had to get through the next few days. Letting out a deep sigh she focused on what lay ahead. She would persevere. She would show him just how determined she could be, that she wasn't just a spoilt, flighty girl.

The clothes Nancy left her were simple; a plain pink cotton dress, but no undergarments. She assumed that was in accordance with Lord Michael's instructions, and did not ask about the lack of a petticoat or drawers when she went downstairs.

She realised she was hungry, which was not surprising since she'd barely eaten any lunch or dinner the previous day, and considering the exhausting and dramatic rigours her body had been put through. When she sat down to eat she felt the mark of the cane acutely, but in a strange way it was comforting. It was a reminder that she was back under his authority and paying for her wayward behaviour.

By the time she finished eating she felt much better, and spent the rest of the morning looking through his library, selecting some books she might read over the following days of her confinement period. She wasn't hungry at midday and so skipped the lunch offered by Nancy, and when the library clock reminded her it was twelve fifty-five she hurried to his study, and then waited outside the door until she heard it chime one o'clock. She wanted to be right on time.

Knocking tentatively she waited, and then heard his voice beckon her. She entered, and saw him sitting at his desk. He stood up, walked past her and closed the door, turning the key in the lock. Without a word he then took her by the arm, walked her to his desk and unceremoniously bent her over it, lifting her dress up onto the small of her back once he was satisfied she was positioned just as he wanted her.

He studied the ridged tramlines of his handiwork. They were almost perfectly formed, and he knew they would

173

still carry quite a smart. Reaching between her legs he touched her, significantly finding the first evidence of moistness on her pouting labia.

She felt so vulnerable and embarrassed, bent and exposed to his whims and fancies as she was. He'd certainly seen her naked charms before, but it was the detached and brooding manner in which he was dealing with her that made her pulse quicken anxiously. She wondered how her punished bottom looked to him, but despite her discomforting predicament, when he touched her pussy lips she wanted to wriggle against his fingers.

But she didn't get the chance to, for he moved away and walked to a cabinet. She stole a glance over her shoulder, and saw he was returning with a crop in his determined grip. Surely he was not going to use that on her, not after what she'd suffered only the day before!

As he had done in the morning, he tapped between her thighs, signalling she should separate her legs. He touched the tongue of the crop against her pussy, and began to lightly tap it, delicately spanking her labia, and then locating and doing the same to her clitoris.

Her unquenched desire from the morning was still upon her, and she responded quickly. She began to writhe lewdly, and to her surprise he did not tell her to stop.

He liked her erotic display. Watching her striped behind moving so salaciously was extremely enjoyable. He already had quite an impressive erection, so he instructed her to close her eyes, and then without missing a beat with the crop, opened his trousers and held his pulsing cock in his free fist. He began to pump himself as he tormented her, avidly watching her twisting, striped bottom as he did so. His first spasm was soon upon him and he relaxed and submitted to it, taking immense pleasure and gratification

174

from the release, and as he ejaculated over her squirming buttocks he heard her panting increase, at the edge of her own moment, and hastily withdrew the teasing crop.

As his breathing calmed he took his handkerchief he wiped his residue from her mouth-watering bottom, and the tip of his wilting penis, then refastened his trousers, but left the tormented girl as she was so he could enjoy the delicious picture for a few more minutes. Feeling quite refreshed from his activities he touched between her legs again, and found her to be very wet – exactly as he wanted her. He moved away and unlocked the door, instructing her to stand up, straighten her clothing and leave.

Elizabeth was in a terrible state. She felt unsteady on her feet, her pussy was tingling and she was light-headed with her craving for release. She took herself straight upstairs to his bedroom, knowing it was forbidden for her to touch herself, but hoping perhaps a lie down might help assuage her suffering.

Without really thinking about it, she instinctively lay on the blanket on the floor, resting her head on the pillow, which was a very wise move for Lord Michael looked in to check on her, wanting to make sure she did not take any liberties with his bed, and to confirm she was not furtively bringing forth her own release.

Later that evening during dinner Elizabeth was reserved and extremely gracious, only speaking when spoken to and granted permission to respond. The simple pink cotton dress suited her mood perfectly, and he enjoyed the way it outlined her shapely figure, leaving nothing to the imagination, and he loved the thought of her wearing no undergarments, easily available to his eye or his hand at any time.

After dinner he told her to take her bath and retire for the night, and later, lying beneath the blanket, she felt a deep tranquillity. This was how she wanted to spend the rest of her life, under Lord Michael's authority, where there were rules and consequences, and a deeply abiding devotion.

When he woke her up she did not know what time it was, but he was sitting on the edge of the bed and he ordered her up and across his lap. She was naked, not having been given a nightdress, and once over his knee he touched between her legs again. She was wet, her lips acutely sensitive to the touch, and using his forefinger and thumb he quickly brought her to the edge of a climax, but as soon as he had her on the brink he cruelly ordered her back on the floor and told her to go back to sleep.

The days that followed conformed to the same format. His teasing switch would wake her, then Nancy would appear with a fresh cotton dress. Frequently she wondered if her clothes had arrived from home, but dare not ask him.

After lunch he would summon her to his study for more tormenting, and after dinner it was straight to her blanket on the floor, only to be disturbed when he retired and left in a state of desperate longing until she fell into a restless sleep. She missed his affection terribly, and she missed his company, for though she was in his house, sleeping next to his bed, he was removed and aloof.

By the third night she was almost in tears from her frustrated state, and during the forth, as she finished her dinner, she wondered how she would be able to get through another night of anguish. It was only one more night, she told herself as she sipped her wine. Just one more night.

'Elizabeth,' he said, startling her out of her reverie, 'I am very pleased with you. You have accepted this period of punishment with fortitude, constraint, and good grace. I am greatly encouraged.'

Elizabeth almost sobbed with joy, her hand trembling as she gracefully put down her wine glass. Her heart began to race and she felt her face flush.

'I am seriously considering, offering you the opportunity to go through an initiation,' he added.

An initiation? What could he mean? She looked at him quizzically but she did not speak, for he had not asked a question nor given her permission to do so.

'An initiation to prove your worthiness,' he elaborated, anticipating her need for more information. 'Perhaps I should become your master, after all,' he pondered.

A little squeal escaped her lips and she looked at him beseechingly. How she longed to serve him, completely and utterly. What was it he had said? He could only be her master if she wanted it utterly.

'You have one last night of your punishment, Elizabeth,' he continued. 'We shall see how you cope with that, and then I'll decide how we proceed from there.'

She wondered why he questioned her ability to cope with another night like the previous few. With such news for inspiration she could endure much more if necessary. She smiled at him, hoping to show him she would not let him down.

'Now go upstairs, take off your dress and wait for me,' he ordered. 'I want you kneeling in front of my armchair by the fireplace, with your hands behind your back.'

Filled with optimism, fighting the desire to throw her arms around his neck and give him a huge kiss, she dashed quickly upstairs, undressed, and positioned herself as he had instructed. She thought he would keep her waiting for quite some time, but he didn't. He was there just moments after she had settled.

He sat in the chair, facing her, his legs languidly parted, his polished shoes by her calves. Without a word he reached out and felt between her thighs, and moved his finger in her wetness to her clit, and within seconds she was panting with need.

'You've been aroused all week, Elizabeth,' he remarked, lifting his glistening fingers from between her legs to her breasts. She sighed deeply as he touched her nipples; it seemed so long since she'd felt his hand there. He caressed and kneaded them, and she moaned with pleasure.

'Would you like to go through the initiation, Elizabeth?' he asked. 'Would you like to see if you have the will and desire to call me your master?'

'Yes, sir,' she replied.

'How badly?'

'Oh very, very badly, sir,' she stressed.

He lowered his fingers back between her legs. 'How can you prove that to me?' he probed, teasing her.

She was almost overcome with desire, finding it difficult to think straight, let alone talk coherently. 'However you wish me to, sir,' she vowed.

He stood up abruptly and pulled the bell cord hanging next to the fire breast.

What was he doing? She looked up, puzzled, but then immediately remembered her place and lowered her eyes respectfully. She'd find out soon enough.

A few minutes passed and Elizabeth was feeling increasingly nervous. Whatever he threw at her, she vowed, she would meet with courage.

Eventually there was a knock on the door and Nancy entered. Elizabeth blushed, and though she desperately wanted to cover her nakedness, she remained obediently as she was.

'Ah, good, Nancy,' he said. 'Come closer. I want you to touch Elizabeth intimately. Let's see if you can bring her to the brink for me.'

'Yes, sir,' Nancy replied, without batting an eye.

Elizabeth was utterly aghast. She looked frantically up at him, but he calmly stared back at her, daring her to rebel.

Nancy knelt beside the distraught girl.

'What was it you were saying, Elizabeth,' he pressed, 'about wanting to prove your desire to partake of the initiation?'

'Oh I do, sir,' she responded hastily, breathlessly, her voice quavering.

Nancy, ignoring the dialogue, touched Elizabeth's sensitive bud, and it took all Elizabeth's self-control not to recoil. She had never even thought about another female touching her and flushed with the intensity of her shame, but she forced herself to stay completely still.

'Elizabeth, you are much too tense,' he gently chided her. 'Take a deep breath and relax. Nancy's not going to harm you. Just feel and savour her touch, in the same way you feel and savour my touch.'

Obediently she filled her lungs and closed her eyes, willing to follow any instructions that may ease her way through such a shameful ordeal. She would pretend it was his skilful touch.

'No, Elizabeth,' he said astutely, 'eyes open. No pretending it's me touching you. That's cheating, and you're not allowed to cheat, are you?'

179

'No, sir,' she gasped shamefully, amazed at his ability to see right through her.

'Look at Nancy's hand touching you, and relish it,' he ordered.

Taking another deep breath Elizabeth did as he said, and despite her anxiety, felt herself surrendering to the knowing, feminine touch. Nancy's intimate contact felt different to his. It was light and danced between her lips like butterfly wings, and in her frustrated state it didn't take long before she was swooning again. This time when she closed her eyes it was not to block out Nancy's touch, but to savour it more acutely.

As she reached her edge, her condition betrayed by a tiny cry and rapid breathing, Nancy removed her fingers but remained kneeling, waiting for further orders from the scrutinising male.

'Very good indeed,' he said approvingly.

Elizabeth sighed in deep frustration, but she was secretly thrilled. She had pleased him, and once more he had proven to be right. She wanted Nancy to touch her again – very much.

'Nancy, remove your blouse and lift your skirt to your waist,' he said.

Elizabeth, eyes downcast, felt a delicious stirring deep inside. It was a sensual curiosity, and suddenly she badly wanted to see Nancy's breasts, almost as much as she wanted Nancy's fingers back between her legs.

'Excellent,' he said, continuing to conduct proceedings. 'Now look up, Elizabeth, and admire Nancy's pretty breasts.'

Elizabeth did look up, just as Lord Michael reached forward and pinched Nancy's nipples. The servant's eyelids fluttered and she let out a little sigh.

'Aren't Nancy's breasts lovely, Elizabeth?' he mused, almost to himself.

'Yes, sir,' she answered sincerely.

'They're a lovely size and shape, aren't they?' he continued, as he held and caressed them. 'So much of them to enjoy, and such a wonderful texture.'

Elizabeth yearned to do just that.

'Wouldn't you just love to touch them, my dear?' He moved one hand from Nancy's breasts to Elizabeth's, and caressed them both in unison.

Elizabeth was sure she would faint with pleasure. 'Y-yes, sir,' she managed, her lips suddenly dry with excitement, and as he continued to fondle her she found it increasingly difficult not to do exactly that.

'Nancy, ask Elizabeth to stroke your breasts.'

'Very good, sir,' Nancy mumbled, turning to the spellbound girl beside her. 'Miss Elizabeth, would you please stroke my breasts?' she whispered, and taking a deep breath, the girl tentatively reached up and experimentally touched the housemaid's erect nipples. Nancy let out a fluttering sigh, and encouraged, Elizabeth moved her hand over the full, plump mound. Lord Michael's fingers were lightly pinching Elizabeth's nipples, so she followed his lead and did the same to her. Nancy began moaning and Elizabeth grew in confidence, coaxed by Lord Michael's caresses, her own simmering desires, and Nancy's alarming but delicious response to her.

'That's enough,' Lord Michael suddenly announced, and Elizabeth, truly disappointed the moment was over, lowered her hand.

'If you're very good, Elizabeth, you'll have many more opportunities to avail yourself of Nancy's luscious body,' he told her, and she looked up at him. Her eyes were alive with her unspent passion, but there was something else there as well – an excitement, a curiosity, a desire to explore and experience more. Lord Michael was very pleased; he had taken her another stage closer.

'You may go, Nancy,' he told the servant. 'Thank you.'

'Thank *you*, sir,' she replied dreamily, and without another word she stood up, straightening her clothes as she left the room.

'No doubt her fingers will be dancing between her legs in five minutes,' he chuckled. 'You'd like that, wouldn't you, Elizabeth? To finally have that release?'

'Yes sir,' she said humbly, frankly. 'I would like that, it is true.'

'But I have said you must wait,' he went on, 'and wait you must. I cannot go back on that, now can I?'

'No, sir,' she replied, knowing he was right.

'And if I did you'd be disappointed, wouldn't you?'

She pondered his question, and concluded that he was right. It was odd, but he was exactly right. She nodded. 'Yes, sir,' she acknowledged. 'I don't quite understand it, but yes, I would be disappointed.'

'Good, it pleases me to hear you say so. Now crawl to your blanket, and tomorrow morning you shall have your moment.'

On her hands and knees, her pussy wet, her breasts still warm from his long awaited touch, she crept submissively across the room. Lord Michael watched her delicious bottom as she did so, and moving behind her, gave her a sharp smack on both cheeks. Not hard enough to sting terribly, but enough for her to feel his hand smartly.

'A little something to send you to bed with,' he said, satisfied. It was far too tempting a target to just let slip by.

Bottom tingling from his hand, frustrated but happy, she settled under her blanket, and fell asleep to thoughts of Nancy's beautiful breasts, and of whatever awaited her on the morrow.

When Elizabeth awoke Lord Michael was sitting on the edge of the bed, looming over her, feet firmly planted apart on the carpet, his very stiff penis in his fist.

'Pull your blanket aside, spread your legs and touch yourself,' he ordered, and transfixed by his fleshy column she immediately did as he ordered and moved her hand between her legs.

'Show me your fingers,' he instructed. 'Still nice and wet,' he observed, 'good. Now stand up and bend over the bed next to me.'

Excited, she rose from the floor and positioned herself as he demanded, next to him, her bottom by his ruddy face. He ran his hand over the smoothly taut cheeks, the stripes just showing the first hints of fading. He raised his hand and spanked her, bringing a bright pink blush to the skin.

'Your bottom should always be red from my hand, and your cunt wet for my cock,' he announced with a crudity that surprised, shocked and thrilled her. He fingered between her legs, his little spanking sending sparks through her loins, his exploring touch electrifying her pussy.

'Next time you feel a need to be disciplined, what will you do, my dear?' he asked, removing his hand. He stood up behind her, and placed his manhood at her wet entrance.

'Tell you, sir,' she gasped, feeling his bulbous knob probing against her.

'That's right. You'll tell me, and I'll decide what method

of punishment you'll receive.'

With that he spanked her again, several times, until she was wriggling salaciously and her bottom was nicely scarlet. Then grabbing her hips he penetrated her to the hilt with one long thrust. She cried out, burying her face in the soft mattress. He felt incredible inside her and she pushed back against him, wanting more.

He fucked her aggressively, fuelled by the passion that had been building in him all week. She wasn't the only one who was in need, and as she attempted to tell him she couldn't control herself, that her moment was nigh, he burst inside her, pumping frantically, and she let out a shriek as a powerful, long awaited orgasm surged through her bent body.

She felt she was bursting into a thousand pieces, so strong were her convulsions. Even after he had become flaccid inside her she continued to spasm, until finally, completely exhausted and totally spent, she collapsed on the enveloping bed.

Chapter Thirteen

The following two days were the happiest Elizabeth had ever known. Her trunk arrived during her punishment period, and Nancy had taken care of her clothes, pressing and hanging them in the guest room.

And it was just as well, for she needed her wardrobe. During the day, while Lord Michael worked, she wandered the shops and lunched with some friends who resided in the city at some very nice cafés. At night Lord Michael took her to dinner, the theatre, even the ballet. Elizabeth behaved admirably, and he rewarded her with light spankings that spread tantalising heat through her nether regions. He also tied her up and made love to her morning and night. He was affectionate and kind, though he remained admirably strict at all times.

Elizabeth, however, could not stop thinking about the promised *initiation*, despite her ongoing mood of contentment. One evening she had just sat down in the sitting room after dinner, wondering if he was planning on taking her out again, when he entered and she looked up at him expectantly.

'So, Elizabeth,' he said, 'you've had a rather splendid time of it over the last couple of days.'

'I have, sir,' she agreed. 'Thank you so much. It's been marvellous.'

'It is clear you've fully recovered from your punishment.'

'I have, sir. Though I'll never forget it.'

'Exactly as it should be. I think it did you the world of good. The cane can be very convincing, along with all other elements of well structured discipline.'

She blushed, for the memory of the cane sent a chill down her spine. In truth it had hurt terribly. 'Yes, sir, I was deserving of every strike. I know that, sir.'

'Yes, you were indeed,' he agreed, sat down next to her, took her hands in his, and ordered her to her knees, causing her heart to skip a beat.

'Now then, have you given any more thought to your proposed initiation?' he asked.

'I didn't need to, sir. There's nothing I wish for more, than to call you my master.'

He nodded and pondered her words. 'Very well, we shall begin tonight. We will be going out, but you need not change your clothes. Just take off all your undergarments, then gather your coat and meet me at the front door.'

Pulse racing, Elizabeth did as he said, and soon they were stepping out into the cool night air. She felt wicked, being out in the streets of London wearing only a dress over her naked body. The carriage was awaiting them, and as it pulled away she suddenly found herself over his knee, wriggling wildly as he spanked her with considerable force.

'I have to make sure you behave yourself tonight, and do exactly as I tell you, Elizabeth,' he said.

'I will, sir,' she cried. 'I promise.'

'Then you can start by being quiet.'

'Yes sir,' she said contritely, accepting the short but sound spanking with fortitude.

He eased her off his lap, made her kneel on the floor of the covered carriage, dress up around her hips, red bottom

186

facing him. She could feel the cold air on her burning, naked flesh, and in the passing streetlamps he could see her sex lips were moist and glistening. Running his hands over the scorched flesh of her buttocks he touched between her lips, found her gratifyingly wet, then pulled her skirt down and helped her sit up next to him. Her face was flushed, her eyes sparkling.

He studied her for a moment, and then cupping her delectable chin in his hands, kissed her affectionately on the lips, a firm but tender kiss that made her toes curl. The discipline and the unexpectedly passionate kiss made her head spin, and she sank into him, surrendering. He silently applauded himself; she was now in the perfect state, both physically and emotionally.

The remainder of the short journey was spent in silence, but by the time the cab came to a halt she was in quite a state.

She looked out the window and found they had stopped in front of a rather unimpressive brownstone. As he stepped down and then helped her out she wondered where on earth they were. At a friend's house?

When they reached the front door he knocked three times, waited, and then knocked three times again. The door creaked open, and she heard the muted sound of laughter and music coming from within. The woman who welcomed them was wearing a rather revealing dress, at least as far as Elizabeth was concerned, but Lord Michael didn't seem to notice.

'Everything is prepared for you, Lord Michael,' the woman said obsequiously, ushering them inside. 'Please, do come this way.'

Nervously clutching Lord Michael's hand, Elizabeth found herself being led down a narrow hallway, carpeted in rich burgundy, the walls adorned with erotic paintings of nudes that made her blush and try to avert her eyes.

The woman showed them into a small but tastefully furnished room, complete with chilled champagne, but the odd thing was – at least Elizabeth thought it odd – there was an armless chair sitting by itself, right in the centre of the floor.

Lord Michael said something to the woman, who turned and left them alone. He then guided Elizabeth to the sofa that squatted against one wall, and without further ado he proceeded to unbutton the front of her dress, pulling it down off her smooth shoulders, leaving her naked from the waist up.

Overcome with his sudden attention she leaned back, closing her eyes, and felt his lips and tongue teasing her nipples and licking her cleavage. She felt his hand pulling up her skirt, and shuddered as his fingers found their way between her pussy lips, teasing her clit again. She was losing herself in the moment, when abruptly he sat up, grabbed her by the hand, and lifted her to her feet. The dress fell from her body and she gasped as he moved her quickly to the chair in the centre of the tiny room, ordering her to sit down and place her hands behind her.

Flushed with the flames of her unsatisfied state it was difficult to focus, but she did as he ordered and he produced some soft rope from somewhere and tied her wrists together.

'Comfortable?' he asked bluntly.

'Yes sir,' she replied, her voice tremulous.

'You're about to experience something quite unique, Elizabeth. Just relax and don't be frightened.'

She felt her heart start to race a little. What was this all about? 'Yes, sir,' she whispered bravely. 'I trust you totally.'

'Remember, this is the first night of your initiation. You must surrender to it, Elizabeth, if you truly wish me to be your master.'

She was terrified but intensely excited.

He dimmed all the lights, and a warm glow fell over the room. He pulled up another smaller chair and placed it to the side of her. She kept waiting for the blindfold, but it never appeared.

He leaned forward and gently kissed her throat. It made her weak with longing, she loved him kissing her, and as his hands caressed her naked breasts she moaned with pleasure.

'Now remember,' he whispered, 'I'm right here with you.'

'Yes, sir,' she murmured, wondering what on earth he meant.

The door creaked open and a beautiful young woman entered. Elizabeth looked at her, puzzled, momentarily forgetting her nakedness, when Lord Michael placed a hand over her mouth.

'Not a word, Elizabeth, just watch,' he whispered firmly.

Filled with trepidation she did so as the girl began to move, humming a song. The few clothes she was wearing began to come off, and she was moving closer to Elizabeth who, transfixed, could not take her eyes off her, though she wanted to tear them away desperately.

As the dance continued Lord Michael continued to whisper reassurances in her ear, continued to kiss her throat and her ear, play with her breasts and tickle her clitoris. The girl drew closer and took off everything except her knickers.

She moved in, touching Elizabeth's breasts, lightly but

definitely. Elizabeth gasped. Nancy was one thing; what happened with her was in the privacy and security of Lord Michael's house, and at least she knew her, but as much as she hated to admit it, Elizabeth felt a strange arousal building. The girl began to pinch her own nipples, and Lord Michael did the same to Elizabeth, who sighed blissfully.

'Isn't she lovely, Elizabeth?' he crooned in her ear. 'Not as lovely as you, but look at her, enjoy her, she's dancing for both of us, but especially for you.'

Elizabeth's head was swirling, her aching need barely overcoming her anxiety. As the lovely young woman continued to move voluptuously Elizabeth gradually began to relax, surrendering to the undeniable heat between her legs.

He felt her reticence waning, and continued kneading her breasts and pinching her nipples. Elizabeth sighed deeply as the dancer spread her legs, straddled Elizabeth's lap, and sat down.

Elizabeth wanted to escape. She also wanted to embrace her. The conflict was utterly confusing. The dancer offered her breasts and pressed them against Elizabeth's.

Elizabeth closed her eyes, and felt the sultry girl cup her breasts. Lord Michael whispered in her ear, ordering her to enjoy it, and Elizabeth moaned as the girl toyed with her. Lord Michael's fingers were at her clit, rubbing with urgency. She felt the girl rise from her lap, and slowly opening her eyes she watched her pick up her clothes and leave the room.

Lord Michael remained next to her, stroking her thighs. Craving more she closed her eyes again, waiting to feel his fingers back on her sex.

'No, not yet,' he said, once again startling her with his

ability to know her thoughts and desires. She wanted to beg for release, but knew she must remain silent.

He continued to tease the insides of her thighs, lightly brushing her labia with his fingers, but never penetrating her. She held her breath, determined to remain compliant, but he stopped and she opened her eyes, dizzy with longing.

'Do you still wish to call me your master?' he asked.

'Y-yes, sir,' she panted.

'Did you like the girl?'

'Yes sir, very much.'

'There may well come a night, my dear, when I will bring you here, just as I did this evening, but instead of going home, as we're doing in a moment, we might join her in a bedroom.'

Elizabeth, filled with need, discovered she wasn't put off by the idea at all.

'How would you feel about that?'

'I think that would be extremely exciting, sir,' she replied honestly.

He was pleased with her open response, untied her, helped her with her dress and led her to the door. The carriage was waiting for them, and settling into the comfortable seat she laid her head back. Though the drive home did not take long, to her it seemed an eternity. She was waiting for him to hold her or touch her again, but he didn't. All he did was clasp her hand reassuringly, which increased her frustration.

At last they were home, and feeling exhausted she gratefully leaned on him as they made their way up the front steps and inside. As soon as he had closed the door he spoke.

'Go upstairs, get undressed, lie on my bed on your back, and wait for me,' he ordered. 'Do not touch yourself.'

She walked up the stairs, too unsure of her step to move quickly, and did as he ordered, hoping he would be upon her quickly – and he was.

He blindfolded her and she felt his naked body against her. He did not bind her wrists or ankles, and she luxuriated in the freedom. He sucked her nipples, rubbing his member against her tummy, then raising his head he whispered, 'I'm very pleased with you, Elizabeth. You did well tonight, so it's time for your reward.'

With an experienced ease of movement he penetrated her, sinking deep as her back arched, and he began to fuck her deliciously. Her mouth opened in a silent scream of ecstasy.

'Clasp your hands together, above your head,' he said, his voice noticeably strained, and she did so, lifting her breasts to meet his roving lips and tongue. Then he rose, turned her over, pulled her to her hands and knees, then grasping her hips he thrust into her again, ordering her to finger herself at the same time, and as soon as she touched her sensitive nubbin she knew she would not be able to hold back for long. His cock filled her pussy and he fucked her with strong, slow, powerful strokes. She let her finger be moved by the thrust of his cock, and as he increased his tempo she felt her moment rapidly approaching.

He felt it too, and she was filled with joy when she heard the command, 'Come for me, Elizabeth!'

She felt him swell inside her as a slow roar began in her ears. The rush began and her explosion started, and with each convulsion she felt him keenly. He was still pumping into her, and the ride continued until finally the swirling momentum ebbed and she flopped back to the bed.

A moment passed, she shivered; the night had a chill to it. He helped her under the covers and cradled her.

'Did I pass, sir?' she whispered tentatively.

'You certainly did, my dear,' he confirmed. 'And now you must rest, for there is more to come.'

She could not think about that, so she sighed happily and let sleep overtake her.

Chapter Fourteen

The following morning Lord Michael roused Elizabeth with a kiss. She stirred, and he whispered that the day was her own. She could sleep in, bathe at her leisure, take a walk, do whatever she wished. At five o'clock, however, she was to go to the guest bedroom.

Elizabeth, still fuzzy from sleep, almost asked why but caught herself in time. She nodded, murmured, 'Yes, sir,' and still feeling drowsy, snuggled back under the covers, grateful for the extra rest.

When she awoke fully she was startled to see it was past eleven. She stretched, looked around the room, and realised she felt nicely refreshed. Clearly such a good night's rest had been greatly needed.

After bathing and dressing she went downstairs, and found Nancy working in the sitting room. She had a twinkle in her eye, but by now Elizabeth knew better than to ask why.

She had a splendid lunch, and then spent the afternoon in the garden reading, enjoying the fresh air. A young kitchen maid brought her afternoon tea at three, and at four-thirty Nancy appeared, telling her she'd best think about coming in.

Upon entering the house Elizabeth thought it seemed oddly quiet. She called out but received no reply, so she went to the sitting room and was relieved to find Nancy straightening the cushions.

'Where is everyone?' she asked.

'Lord Michael and the rest of the staff are out,' Nancy replied. 'They'll be gone all evening, as will I. In fact, I should have left already.'

'But I don't understand – is something the matter?' Elizabeth asked.

'There's nothing the matter, and I'm sure things will become clearer as the evening progresses.'

Elizabeth caught her breath. This was about her continuing initiation, she was sure. For some reason Lord Michael wanted the house empty. A shiver of excitement ran down her spine as she tried to imagine why. What was she in for now?

'You'd best ready yourself for the evening and get to the guestroom,' Nancy said, reminding her of Lord Michael's earlier words.

So after her bath, dressed in just a robe, she made her way to the designated room. She felt quite peculiar, being alone in the house. Cautiously she opened the door, and not seeing or hearing anything amiss, slipped into the bedroom. Once inside she noticed some clothes laid out, and an envelope with her name on it sat prominently in the centre of the bed.

As she took a closer look at the dress she let out a little cry. It was a maid's uniform, but not like any she'd ever seen before. The black skirt was very short indeed, and she could not see any sort of a blouse; just a little frilly white apron with an attached bib that would barely cover her breasts. The little cap was sweet enough, but there were also frilly cuffs and a collar. She sat down on the bed, and with shaking fingers opened the envelope.

In Lord Michael's distinctly meticulous hand, she read:
Elizabeth,
An old school friend will be joining me for dinner this

evening. His name is Sir Andrew, but you are only to refer to him as 'sir'. You are to show him the same respect you show me.

You will dress as our maid, in the uniform provided. We will be dining out, but upon our return you are to be fully prepared to see to any requirements we may have. There will be no other members of my staff present, as they have been given the evening off, so all responsibilities concerning the comfort of my guest will end with you.

You will station yourself in the kitchen, but be prepared to commence your duties, beginning with drinks in the sitting room, at six precisely.

Lord Michael.

Elizabeth stared at the note, read it again, and then a third time. She took off the robe, slipped into the skirt, the apron and the cuffs, and studied her reflection in the full-length mirror on the wardrobe. It was positively scandalous.

The bib did cover her breasts, but only just, her cleavage and their outer curves remaining clearly visible for anyone to admire. And the skirt was just *so* short!

If it were just Lord Michael she was serving she'd have been thrilled at the prospect, but he was bringing a friend. How could she possibly present herself in such a fashion? With trembling fingers she tied the lacy collar around her throat.

She looked down at her naked legs. Were there no stockings? Searching the bed she breathed a sigh of relief when she found them under her robe. Sadly though, when she had finished rolling them up her legs, she found the lacy tops were visible a few inches below the hem of the skirt.

She flopped on the bed. This couldn't be possible! Surely Lord Michael wouldn't want her to appear in such an outrageous outfit in front of another man? But if this is what he had left for her, then this is what he wanted. It was as simple as that. But could she go through with it? Summoning every ounce of courage, taking a deep breath, she busied herself with her hair, then some lipstick and rouge. If she was going through with this she would look her best.

She looked around for shoes but could not find any. Apparently he wanted her in her stocking feet, and as she made her way downstairs to the kitchen she had to admit the lack of shoes was definitely humbling.

She'd only been waiting anxiously for a few minutes when she froze as a loud tinkling startled her. She looked up. The bell cord in the sitting room was being pulled. It was time to begin her duties. Hurriedly she scurried along the hall, suddenly wondering if she should have already been there waiting for them.

Nervously she knocked, and entered when called. Lord Michael was standing by the fire, and his dinner companion was sitting on the couch. She shot a furtive glance at the stranger, and was unsettled to note that he certainly was not a particularly attractive man.

'Elizabeth, a sherry for the both of us, and a smack for you,' Lord Michael said snootily. 'You should have been waiting for us, ready to serve.'

Elizabeth felt her face burn with embarrassment and she silently cursed herself for realising that requirement too late, and then quickly moved to the occasional table to pour their drinks, finding it a little difficult to control her trembling fingers. Picking up the silver tray she offered the first glass to Lord Michael, then nervously offered the other to his guest. She felt naked as she lowered the tray, and though she dared not look at him directly, she could feel his eyes devouring her cleavage. She did not like his unwanted attention, and it made her shiver.

'Thank you, my dear girl,' he whined as he accepted the drink, and she didn't get a nice feeling about him at all.

'Thank you, sir,' she replied demurely, then forced herself to bob a little curtsy.

'Put the tray back and come here, Elizabeth,' Lord Michael said sternly, so she hurried to the occasional table, replaced the tray where it was, and returned to him. 'Put your hands up on the mantelpiece,' he ordered.

Flushed with complete embarrassment, she raised her arms and did as he said.

'You should have been here, waiting to serve us,' he repeated. 'You will now receive two smacks to concentrate your mind.'

'Yes sir, thank you, sir,' she gasped, her face scarlet with shame. To her horror he lifted her skirt, rendering her bare bottom completely exposed for the strange man to scrutinise.

She cast her tormentor a wide-eyed look of pleading, which was completely ignored by him, and then she stiffened as the palm of his hand landed with a loud smack and a sharp sting. First he spanked one cheek and then the other, asking once the brief but sharp reprimand was completed, 'Do you still want me to be your master, Elizabeth?'

'Yes sir,' she replied stoically.

He nodded, satisfied with her response. 'That will be all for now,' he said, in his usual tone of voice. 'We shall ring if we need anything.'

'Yes sir, thank you, sir,' she said humbly, and head bowed, face burning, she left the room.

As soon as she reached the kitchen she slumped on one of the wooden chairs. Had she ever felt so embarrassed in her entire life? How would she ever get through the evening with that odious little man there witnessing her continuing humiliation?

She found a bottle of red wine and dared pour herself a small glass, hoping it might help to calm her nerves. After a sip or two she began to relax, and thought some more about the guest.

Lord Michael had said his name was Sir Andrew, and from her surreptitious glance she noted red hair, cold blue eyes, and a hawk nose; not a person she would care to spend time with, she decided.

Then it suddenly dawned on her that it was a fellow by the name of Sir Andrew who owned the house in which they stayed all too briefly up north. She wondered if he was the very same, and concluded that of course he must be. For some reason the thought comforted her and she felt a little more confident; having stayed in the man's house, he seemed less of a stranger and consequently his presence less disconcerting.

Four hours later the little wine she'd found had gone, and as the bell at last jingled again, her brief resurgence of confidence evaporated with it. Feeling weary and anxious she went to the sitting room, where Lord Michael was standing with his back to the fire, and Sir Andrew was lounging in the armchair nearby. Both men were contentedly puffing on large cigars.

'Ah, there you are; I was beginning to think you'd fallen asleep on duty,' Lord Michael said, a little sarcastically, and Sir Andrew sniggered tipsily. 'But now you're here we would both like a large brandy to round off the splendid dinner we've enjoyed at my club.'

'Yes, sir,' she replied, and proceeded to pour the amber liquid from the crystal decanter into the brandy glasses on the sideboard, before placing them on the small silver tray and serving the two gentlemen.

'Will there be anything else, sir?' she asked.

'Yes,' he said frankly, 'you will take hold of the mantelpiece, and move your feet back and apart slightly.'

Her face burned anew, but she summoned her resolve and reminded herself to obey, not think.

'And since Sir Andrew is my guest, I think he should have the honour,' Lord Michael decreed.

She shuddered. This was all too much, but despite her misgivings she obeyed, inching her feet back and apart, having to lean forward a little, her back straight and the tendons in her thighs and calves tensed. The fire warmed her front, and she knew her position had caused her short skirt to rise slightly, fearing the lower curves of her buttocks were now visible.

'Ah, that's better,' Sir Andrew mused approvingly.

'I could not agree more,' Lord Michael concurred wholeheartedly, admiring the deliciously shapely body leaning against the fireplace beside him.

'Excellent,' Sir Andrew mumbled around his fat cigar. 'What a delightful picture she makes, and no mistake.'

Elizabeth felt herself blush; she was being displayed for their gratification like an exhibit at a gallery.

'Feet a little further apart,' Lord Michael instructed, taking a sip of his brandy and then placing the sparkling crystal beside her splayed fingers on the mantelpiece.

She obeyed, cringing inwardly at the way she was being

200

manipulated, emotionally and physically, for the pleasure of the two men. Then she heard the soft chink of lead crystal being placed on mahogany, and the subtle creak of leather as the guest adjusted his position, leaning forward, and she held her breath, awaiting the inevitable.

'I believe a degree of correction is required, my good friend,' the man said, 'for being neglectful of her duties upon our return from your club.'

'And I would agree,' Lord Michael said.

There was a tense pause, when the only sound in the room was the crackling fire, and then a cold hand touched her bottom.

'Such a splendid rump,' he said, and Lord Michael nodded.

'It most certainly is,' he agreed proudly.

Elizabeth was mortified; Sir Andrew's chilly touch was crawling over her exposed bottom, and they were discussing her as though she wasn't even there!

'You've done a remarkable job in taming this one in such a relatively short period of time,' Sir Andrew said, complimenting his friend.

'We've a long way to go yet,' Lord Michael replied.

'And I would be more than happy to help, should you need a hand,' he sniggered, amused at his pun. 'Now let's see,' he went on, his demeanour serious once again, 'I think a few good smacks,' he decided, raising his hand, and Elizabeth gasped and clutched the mantelpiece tighter as it swept down and pounded her vulnerable bottom, the severe impact causing the tensed cheeks to quiver enticingly. 'Her bottom is so much prettier when adorned with the marks of a just punishment,' he commented, slapping her again, then building into a rhythm that had Elizabeth screwing her face up in anguish and rocking towards the mantelpiece with each fresh impact. But she gritted her teeth and withstood the onslaught, desperately wanting it to cease whilst taking the humiliating punishment with fortitude.

'And for good measure, my favourite spot,' Sir Andrew panted, his efforts rendering him a little out of breath, running the palm of his hand up and down the insides of Elizabeth's thighs, 'four good smacks on each side. And this will sting more acutely, believe me, young lady.'

Elizabeth held her breath, and the palm that swatted against her inner thigh did indeed carry a fierce bite. The four spanks almost dragged the tears from her tightly closed eyes, but she fought them back, the creamy flesh of her thighs surprisingly more sensitive than that of her bottom, and by the time the eight smacks had been applied she was almost at the end of her tether, pushed to her limits by the lateness of the hour and the fact that it was not Lord Michael dispensing the punishment – the latter compounded by the fact that she instinctively disliked the arrogant bully.

Having bid his friend goodnight and seen him out to the waiting cab, Lord Michael returned to the sitting room, sat down on the sofa, and told Elizabeth to kneel on the carpet before him, hands behind her back.

'That was a big night for you, my dear,' he said, brushing her fringe up off her flushed brow, 'and you did remarkably well. I am very pleased and proud of you. Your training is not just physical; you are being tested at every level, mental and emotional, and you are progressing very nicely.' He puffed on his cigar and finished the last drop of his brandy. 'Now go upstairs and get to bed. I'll be up shortly, but tonight we sleep. You've earned a good night's rest.'

'Thank you, sir,' she said softly, rising with her usual elegant grace, padding across the floor in her stocking feet and leaving the room with a pretty backward glance at him.

To date she had far surpassed all his expectations, and now she had just one more night to go.

The following evening Elizabeth sat expectantly on the couch in the sitting room. He had told her earlier in the day her initiation was almost over, and to wait for him after dinner.

She hadn't seen him since then, dining alone and now feeling rather fidgety, awaiting his return.

She heard the front door open and close, and caught her breath. Her pulse quickened as she heard him hand his coat and hat to Nancy.

When he entered the room she wasn't sure if she should remain sitting, stand up and greet him, or kneel, and so feeling unsure of herself she decided to take the safest route, and dropped to her knees.

He smiled. 'Excellent. Your instincts are improving.'

'Thank you, sir,' she replied, blushing with pride rather than embarrassment or shame.

He sat on the couch in front of her and took her hands in his. 'I have some good news, Elizabeth,' he said. 'Tonight is the final night of your initiation.'

'I hope I will not disappoint you, sir.'

'I am sure you'll do very well. You've not let me down thus far, so I've no reason to assume otherwise now. Are you ready to begin?'

'Yes, sir,' she answered determinedly, though not sure exactly what she was supposed to be ready for.

'Very well. You will go upstairs, bathe, and wait for me,

kneeling by my chair.'

She nodded and stood up quickly, a sudden wave of tension rendering her unable to utter another word.

Upstairs in his bedroom she nervously began to prepare herself, wondering what lay ahead, what discipline she might have to suffer.

By the time she had her lustrous hair brushed and lipstick applied her nervousness was palpable, her entire being tingling with anticipation.

Lord Michael took his time, finished his evening paper, enjoyed a brandy, then leisurely made his way up the stairs and found her waiting as instructed. She looked appropriately tense as he slowly moved to his chair and sat down.

'So, my sweet Elizabeth, you still wish to call me your master?'

'Yes sir, very much,' she said sincerely.

'Before we begin, I want to make sure you understand that if I am your master you will be under my authority at all times, for as long as you serve me. Is that what you really want, Elizabeth?'

'It is, sir, yes,' she insisted.

'You wish to be subject to my total control and discipline?'

'Yes, sir.'

'Do you understand that I will spank you when I wish, I will fuck you as I please, and you must obey me at all times in all things?'

'Yes, sir,' she said, 'I do.'

'For instance,' he pressed, 'if I become your master, you will not be permitted to wear undergarments. You've already experienced that for a few days, but I shall require their absence each and every day. I will have you naked under your clothes at all times.'

The thought of constantly being secretly undressed sent a little shiver down her spine. It was such a wicked concept. She nodded meekly.

'Although I may decide to corset you,' he pondered.

She was supposed to wear corsets for certain of her dresses, but had refused when living at home. She thought about the confining undergarment, and could easily understand why he would have her in such a thing; a corset worn for him would be a far different matter.

'Very well,' he said, breaking into her thoughts, 'your last night of initiation will begin. If you get through the next few hours I will make you mine, as only a true master can.'

She shivered a little; the last remark sounded ominous, but before she could give it much thought his voice claimed her attention once again.

'First, my dear, you will learn the five positions. Position one, is what you are doing now. Kneeling, knees slightly apart – a little more than they are, please… that's better. Hands behind your back, head lowered, eyes downcast. When I tell you to assume position one, that is what you do. Is that clear?'

'Yes, sir.'

'Position two, on your hands and knees, bottom facing me. Assume it now.'

Elizabeth placed her hands flat on the carpet and shuffled around.

'Very nice…' he mused, admiring her bottom. 'Now, position three, drop to your elbows and touch your cheek to the carpet. Make sure you dip your back so your bottom is nicely raised.'

She did as he instructed, and he viewed the delicious

sight with immense satisfaction.

'Position four, reach back, hands on your bottom and spread yourself, my dear.'

She cringed, for it still humiliated her to do this, but obediently she took her weight on the side of her face, placed her hands on her buttocks and eased them apart. So delectable did she look that he was unable to resist, and leant forward to inquisitively probe her tiny puckered star with a forefinger, enjoying her soft gasp, muffled slightly by the carpet.

'Excellent,' he said, his voice slightly thick. 'You will be told to do this regularly, so you had better get used to it.'

'Yes sir,' she whispered, her voice tremulous. 'I'll try my best, sir.'

'Position five, the last, is spread-eagled on the floor.'

Immediately and gratefully she moved her hands and spread herself out.

'Legs wider,' he ordered, and she spread them as wide as she could, and then waited. 'Have you memorised what I've just taught you?'

'Yes sir, I think so,' she replied.

'Well, let's test you, shall we?'

He called out the various positions by number only, in random order, and Elizabeth moved into each one correctly and decisively. Satisfied, he had her finish with her least favourite, position four, telling her not to move until he gave his permission.

Elizabeth was mortified by his command, but it wasn't painful or uncomfortable, just utterly humiliating. She had to admit, though, that it did make her feel completely submissive, and recognised that was the important point. But then only when she felt the cool lubricant being applied to her anus did she realise that the intense sense of submission was only a small part of the agenda.

'You will be accommodating this for a while,' he said, and began to ease the dildo into her tight, resisting back passage. She tensed and he spanked her, causing her to squeal with the shock of the blow. 'Relax and accept it!' he barked.

As always his command made the difference, and she felt herself accept the intruder. He moved it in and out a few times, then sank it deep and left it embedded there, the base just visible between her soft buttocks.

He instructed her to kneel up and face him, and she saw he was holding two pieces of rope. One he wrapped around her waist, cinching it tightly, securing it with a knot. The other he tied to the first, and she realised that he planned to tighten it between her legs. She gasped as the rope dug between her pussy lips. He told her to turn around, and then he pulled the rope up. It pressed against the base of the dildo and he knotted it tightly to her waist rope.

'There,' he mused with satisfaction, 'very nice, too. It is called a rope harness, my dear, and it holds the artificial penis in your bottom rather nicely, don't you think?'

'Y-yes, sir,' she managed, mortified with shame.

'It will also infuriate your sweet clitoris until I remove it,' he elaborated. 'Isn't that clever, too?'

The night was young – what else did he have in store for her?

'Now then, I have three very good friends to whom I am going to introduce you,' he continued. 'Remain kneeling as you are.'

Panic rose in her chest, catching her breath. The experience with Sir Andrew had been bad enough, *three* strange men would be unbearable!

'Position two,' he said, and immediately she moved onto her hands and knees.

'This, Elizabeth, is my friend the strap.' She breathed a huge sigh of relief. 'Relieved are you, that I wasn't talking about more of my male acquaintances?'

'Yes, sir,' she answered, knowing she had to be completely honest.

'You understand, don't you, that if I choose to share you amongst my friends you must comply? You do understand this, don't you, Elizabeth?'

'Yes, sir,' she answered, blushing at the thought, 'I do understand.'

'But we are in danger of getting distracted from the matter at hand,' he said resolutely. 'We must continue. As I was saying, this is my loyal strap.' He placed the cool implement against her bottom. 'Do you feel it, my dear? It is stout leather, with rounded edges so as not to break your skin. I am told it has quite a smart to it. If I should become your master there will be occasions when I decide to give you a thorough strapping. It may be simply for good measure, or because you require such a punishment, or simply because I want to for my own enjoyment. Do you understand?'

'Yes, sir.'

'Good. Now I shall apply two strokes to your bottom so you may officially meet him. Are you ready, young lady?'

She nodded, suddenly unable to speak again.

'Remember, this is not a punishment. It is an introduction. Now assume position three.'

She lowered to her elbows and placed her cheek against the carpet, dipping her back to lift her bottom for him.

He stood up, and lightly tapped the custom leather belt against her left buttock. Then raising it, he lashed it down sharply. The leather cracked against her skin, creating an impressive sight and sound, and she struggled to suppress a hiss.

He walked around her, placing it on her right buttock, then repeated the action, applying the same amount of force, and she fought the rapid evacuation of her lungs again.

'What do you think of my reliable friend, my dear?' he asked, almost congenially.

'He is very effective, sir,' she muttered, gasping against the sharp sting.

'Yes, he can be. Now face me, position one.'

Bottom smarting, Elizabeth knelt up, the rope rubbing between her buttocks and thighs, the dildo wedging tighter inside her, and faced him, hands behind her back.

Bending a little and cupping one of her breasts, he lifted its firmness slightly. 'They really are a perfect pair of titties, Elizabeth,' he said admiringly. 'And you enjoyed touching Nancy's titties the other evening, didn't you?' Her coy blush only served to confirm what he already knew about the girl. He straightened and continued, reiterating, 'Remember, Elizabeth, when I give you an instruction I do not expect to see any hesitation whatsoever. I expect you to obey my orders instantly and without question.' There was a warning timbre to his voice and she nodded immediately, the rope around her waist and between her legs a constant distraction. Every movement caused it to stimulate her clitoris and gently manipulate the dildo in her tight rear passage, stoking her traitorous excitement inexorably.

He toyed with the strap as he gazed at her naked charms,

and Elizabeth eyed it with angst, her sparkling eyes following its movements in his grip.

'Lift your chin a little, my dear,' he instructed, 'and present your breasts for me with pride.'

Filled with trepidation she did so, knowing she had no other choice but to obey, pulling her shoulders back and thrusting her breasts forward to the mercy of whatever he desired.

The leather strap lifted and then swept down with vicious accuracy, catching her directly across both her poor nipples, causing her to shriek with the pain and rock back on her heels.

'Hmmm…' he said pensively, watching the ruddy blotchiness tint her fleshy globes. 'That looks delightful, my dear. Very pleasing indeed.' And then the strap lifted a second time and struck her with a *splat!* that resounded around the room, the sound of leather on flesh and her squeal of dismay, and the sight of her quivering breasts and anguished expression, satisfying him immensely.

'Excellent,' he mused, and then the strap struck again, and a fourth, fifth and sixth time. Elizabeth was in a state of emotional and physical torment, but he was delighted to see her hands remained clutched behind her back, not moving an inch to defend herself from the onslaught. Her demeanour was utterly obedient and submissive, and even her gasping protests fell silent.

Lord Michael stopped the beating, laid the strap on the nearby chest-of-drawers, then rubbed both Elizabeth's breasts with his cupped hands, a dreamy sigh escaping her lips.

'That is very good,' he murmured.

'Thank you, sir,' she whispered, her voice husky, and despite her self-consciousness she found herself engulfed by his attention.

'And so, it's time to move on,' he told her. 'You must now learn what pleasures your mouth and lips and tongue can afford me. But first I want you to assume position two.'

Dutifully, totally submissive in manner, she turned around and rested on all fours, then felt him undo the rope between her legs. At last it was coming off, but rather than remove it he simply loosened and pulled it to one side. Taking hold of the dildo he began to move it in and out, and she moaned, dropping her forehead to the carpet as the hedonistic practices continued.

'Wriggle for me,' he commanded, slapping her red rump, and she obeyed again, squirming salaciously and rolling her hips.

'That's better. I want to see you enjoy this.' He reached down and teased her labia and she responded, thrusting against his hand, pushing back against the dildo.

'Good...' he crooned, 'just a little more. Show me how you can fuck it, my dear little slut.' She cringed at the humiliating order, but dipping her back she ground her bottom onto the artificial penis, inwardly begging for more.

'Good... that's very good,' he complimented her. 'Now remain absolutely still.' Elizabeth moaned as he slowly withdrew it from her, and then caught her breath when he declared, 'Time to move up another size, I believe.'

Elizabeth could not believe her ears! Surely he wasn't about to penetrate her bottom again, with something even larger! She winced as she felt him apply some additional lubrication to ease the rude insertion, and a moment later he was pressing the stout artificial penis into her. She did her best to relax and accept it, but for a while her sphincter resisted, and then letting out a long deep breath, she felt it loosen a little and surrender. Slowly but surely he pushed, and soon her bottom was completely impaled again, stretched tightly around the inert trespasser.

'Position one,' he said, and she straightened up quickly, feeling the rope being pulled tightly between her smarting buttocks and knotted once again. The new dildo felt huge inside her.

'That's very good indeed,' he said. 'Now then, time to meet another of my good friends, and then we'll proceed with the next of your lessons.' He paused and scrutinised her pensively. 'Assuming you wish to continue the initiation. You do wish to continue, don't you, Elizabeth?'

'Y-yes, sir,' she muttered wearily. 'V-very much, sir.'

'Position three,' he announced, and she lowered her forearms to the floor. 'This is my flogger, or cat 'o nine tails,' he informed her, holding the whip for her to see, then draping the leather tongues across her pink, raised bottom. 'It delivers a sharp burn, and is quite different to the results induced by the strap. Are you ready to receive it?'

'Um, yes sir,' she replied. 'I think so, sir. If it pleases you.'

'Good. It is anxious to make your acquaintance, too. Crawl up onto the bed and adopt position five, with a pillow under your tummy.'

'There,' he said with satisfaction as soon as she'd completed his instructions, gazing down at the delicious image before him, her bottom perfectly positioned and an exquisite target to enjoy, 'that's perfect... just perfect.' The whip moved back, the handle in one hand, the gathered strands held together in the other. 'Remember, my dear, this is neither punishment nor discipline – this is an introduction. If you want me as your master you must taste some of what you'll be facing.'

'Yes, sir,' she answered timorously, not sure she was ready for what was coming.

'Are you ready?'

'Yes, sir, I think so,' she said again, and then the leather strips snapped through the air and hit her raised bottom with a *thwacking* sound. She buried her face in the coverlet to stifle her cry, and then tried to absorb the deep, powerful burning.

'Ready for number two?' he asked.

'Yes, sir,' she mumbled sorrowfully, unaware she was swaying her hips in a futile attempt to assuage the scalding pain. Repeating the exact method he let the flogger loose, and she clenched her teeth as the scalding tongues bit deep again.

'A sound flogging leaves a strong impression,' he remarked as he moved back to his chair, picked up the strap, and returned it and the flogger to the dresser. 'Wouldn't you agree, my dear?'

'Yes, sir,' she replied, her voice quaking. 'I have no doubt about that.' Across her taut flesh she could feel the scorched imprints of the leather tongues, and she could hardly imagine what it would be like to receive numerous lashes, one after the other.

'Now then, about your pretty mouth...' He moved back to the bed and sat on the edge next to her, admiring her red rump and his handiwork that had achieved such a gratifying result. The flogger had left a delightful pattern, and he could not resist tracing his hand over it, smoothing the ridged flesh, enjoying her little gasp as he did so.

'Lips...' he reflected, 'lips are such lovely sensuous things, my dear, and you must learn how to use yours in order to give me the utmost pleasure.' He moved his hand, tracing the sensuous outline of her pouting mouth with his fingertips. 'You will always remember what a privilege it is to suck me. Do you understand what I am saying to you?' Her endearing expression told him she suspected, but wasn't quite sure or able to accept it. 'Suck my finger as you think I would like you to suck my penis,' he told her, and eased his straightened forefinger between her lips, deep into her mouth, and she instinctively moved her head back and forth and sucked, her cheeks hollowing with a promise that made his cock flex in his trousers. Entwining the fingers of his free hand in her silky hair he guided her, faster or slower, as was his whim at any one moment. Satisfied she had a natural ability for the task, he withdrew his glistening finger.

'Now then,' he said, shifting his weight fractionally so he could open his trousers, lower them a little and move his shirttails aside, his sturdy erection bobbing up from the shadows of his groin before her spellbound face. 'Is there something you wish to ask me, my dear?' he coaxed, eager to feed his cock into her warm wet mouth.

Elizabeth stared at it, pulsing powerfully before her sparkling eyes, knowing exactly what was expected of her. 'P-please, sir,' she quietly ventured, 'it would be an honour and a privilege to suck it for you. Please may I suck it?'

'You may, my dear,' he consented. 'Indeed you may.'

Elizabeth shuffled a little closer and lowered her head. She tried to imagine it was his finger again, for her technique then seemed to please him. She gingerly took the bulbous head into her mouth, then formed a tight seal with her lips and sucked, her tongue fluttering nervously against his gnarled underside, her flushed face sinking lower towards his hairy groin. She could feel him swelling even further and feared he would be too big for her, that her jaw couldn't take his girth, and then she tasted a little seepage of semen on her tongue.

'You are doing well, my dear,' he praised her, his voice strained. 'But if I am to become your true master you will have to welcome my ejaculation into your mouth. Is that a problem for you, Elizabeth?'

With her lips stretched and her mouth full, all she could manage was a little hum and a faint shake of her head, which Lord Michael actually found a heady stimulus that had his fingers clutching her hair tightly as he fought against the threat of an early conclusion to his pleasure, and an untimely end to her initiation.

She managed another hum and a stilted nod.

'Very good. But for now I must resist the delights of your mouth and save that particularly enjoyable practice for another time, hugely tempting though it is to continue and christen your throat.

'Now, adopt position four, Elizabeth.'

She released the erection from her oral clutches and moved for him, and sighed with relief as he undid the knot and finally removed the chafing rope. She lowered her head, resting her cheek in the mattress, and placing her hands on her buttocks she spread them apart. Now, perhaps, she would at last be rid of the dildo.

Lord Michael moved behind her, kneeling between her parted thighs. Then taking the base of the rude shaft he began to slide it in and out, whilst teasing her clitoris with his other hand. She was so excited, so turned on by the events of the evening, she began grinding back against his artful fingers, aching for her orgasm, and the stout column was suddenly a part of her arousal rather than an uncomfortable intruder. She was nearly there when he slowed the pace, and then withdrew the dildo completely. Withdrawing his hand from between her legs he touched her puckered portal.

'Hmm, nicely prepared,' he adjudged.

If I am to become your master, Elizabeth, you must give yourself to me in every way.' Elizabeth pondered the word 'if'. Had she not proven time and again how much she longed for him? How much she wanted him to be her master? The greasy lubricant being applied to her anus for the third time that evening concentrated her mind. 'You have done exceptionally well tonight, my dear girl,' he said, but you have one last hurdle to surmount.' She tensed, sensing something bigger than anything she'd encountered thus far. 'I told you previously there was an ultimate surrender; something even more significant than the taking of your maidenhead. Do you remember me telling you that?'

'Yes sir, I do,' she replied, her voice soft, filled with uncertainty.

'It will fill you with a sense of complete submission, and make you feel truly and totally owned by me. Do you know what I intend, Elizabeth?'

He touched her lubricated portal with his bulbous knob, and she gasped with mixed emotions.

Surely he didn't mean…?

But she knew he did.

'Yes sir,' she whispered. 'I do know what you intend.'

'If you truly want me to be your master, then I must take you as a master takes his slave. Do you still wish to serve me, Elizabeth? Do you want to submit utterly? Do you want to offer me your ultimate surrender?'

Her hands were still holding her soft cheeks apart, and she closed her eyes in resignation and nodded against the mattress, recognising the fulfilment of his demand as the ultimate surrender she could offer him.

He pressed a little more insistently, probing for an answer.

'Yes sir,' she gasped. 'Please take me as a master takes his slave, and accept my total submission.'

'Very well, but one last question, and then I will accept your most precious gift and consummate our union.'

Another question? What could it possibly be?

'Why do you wish me to be your master, Elizabeth?'

Of all the questions he had put to her, of all the tests she'd been given, this was the easiest of them all, and without hesitating she replied, 'Because I love you, my lord.'

He clutched her hips.

The desire to submit, the courage to explore, the ability to understand, none of this meant anything without her adoration, devotion, and love.

He pushed forward with his hips and sank inside her tight, hot depths. Elizabeth felt the stretch, and after a brief moment of panic, she managed to relax and accept him. She was overwhelmed, and as he'd promised, felt herself being swept away by an intense, flowing sense of submission as he kept pressing inward, his rigid cock filling her until she was completely impaled upon it.

'Move your hands,' he said, and she allowed them to drop to her sides, her fingers clutching the bedcover, feeling her buttocks close snugly around him. Leaning forward, covering her dipped back and exulting in the feel of her taut bottom cocooned tightly against his groin, he whispered in her ear, 'You belong to me now, Elizabeth. You're mine, completely and utterly.'

'Yes, master,' she gasped, sobbing as she uttered the

words.

He straightened up, and slowly began to pump between her cheeks, squeezing and moulding them around his fleshy piston. He returned his teasing fingers to her clit, toying in her wetness, and all the while her snug rectum gripped him exquisitely.

Intoxicated by the joy of his acceptance, her deep sense of surrender, the emotional release of expressing her love, the electrifying touch of his fingers, and the omnipotent presence of his cock taking her from behind in the most wicked of places, Elizabeth felt the onset of a powerful and profound orgasm. She was sobbing from it all, and as he pumped more aggressively, as his fingers coaxed more vigorously, she felt the massive wave upon her.

'Oh, master…' she wailed.

'Come for me, my sweet slave,' he urged through gritted teeth. 'Come for me, Elizabeth!'

Her muscles tensed, gripping him even more, and suddenly he felt his seed surging. The huge wave washed over her and she cried out as the convulsion gripped her. As the next spasm rippled through her she suddenly felt herself floating, the orgasm flashing coloured lights behind her tightly closed eyelids. Her pussy was pulsating, pulsing with pleasure, and then very slowly the blissful sensations subsided, as did her drained body into the mattress.

She felt him slip out of her, lie by her side, pulling her to him and cradling her in his arms. She was sobbing quietly and he remained silent, holding her close, letting her shed the energy and emotion of the moment.

'Master,' she finally whispered, then looked up at him.

'My sweet Elizabeth,' he said. 'I am happy that you belong to me. But rest now, for in the morning I have something very special for you.'

Prologue

In accordance with his instructions, Elizabeth was dressed only in a white silk robe tied with a sash at her waist. Her hair was up, and she was kneeling by his chair, waiting.

He had made glorious love to her when they awoke, but this time he plundered her pussy, and holding her hands above her head, pumped until they were both gasping from their sudden intense explosions.

Now, after bathing and dressing as he instructed, she was waiting patiently, utterly jubilant at the turn of events. He was busy in his closet, and finally turned and walked over to her. He was carrying two boxes, and sat down in his chair, smiling at her.

'You look very happy, Elizabeth,' he remarked.

'Oh, master, I am,' she replied, her elation evident in her wide, sparkling eyes.

'I have two presents for you,' he said, indicating the boxes.

'Presents?' she beamed excitedly, thinking of the silver music box he had bought her, now her most precious possession. 'Thank you, master.'

He opened the top box and withdrew a black velvet case, and she caught her breath, for as far as she was concerned only jewellery came in such packaging.

He lifted the lid and she saw a gold rope chain, in the centre of which was a black and white cameo, surrounded by a thick gold band. Her eyes widened in awe. It was one of the most beautiful things she had ever seen.

'Master,' she gasped, 'for me?'

'Yes, Elizabeth, it is for you, and it is very special. This is your collar, and you must never take it off.'

Mesmerised, gratefully absorbing his words, she watched as he reverently lifted the gold necklace out of its case.

'As you can see, the clasp is quite unique,' he went on. 'When I remove this tiny rod it locks in place. It cannot be unclasped unless the rod is put back. It is like a key. I shall have the rod, Elizabeth, and only I will be able to remove your collar. Do you understand me?'

'Yes, master,' she replied, gazing at her wonderful collar.

'Look closely at the cameo,' he instructed. 'What do you think it is?'

She stared at the white image against the black background. It appeared to be two roses, side by side, their thorns barely discernible.

'Are they roses, master?' she asked.

He nodded. 'Yes, it does appear so, doesn't it? A rose is rather like what we share, don't you think? So sweet and beautiful, but with thorns to prick when needed.'

The analogy was not lost on her.

'As you can see, there's a similar rod at the top of the cameo, and if I remove it,' he said, doing so, 'the cameo snaps out. Like this.' He removed the cameo, leaving the gold band empty. 'Why do you think I had it designed this way, Elizabeth?'

She stared at the hollow ring, but could not figure it out. 'I'm sorry, master,' she said, feeling a little deflated for appearing to be a little obtuse, 'but I don't know.'

'For this,' he told her, and reaching back inside the box, he retrieved a delicate leash, woven from gold thread, with a snap-clasp at one end that he attached into the empty gold ring. 'It forms a collar and leash for my pet slave,' he explained.

'Oh, my goodness!' she exclaimed.

'There are some special events we will attend, during which you will need to be on a collar and leash. And it is my intention that you shall have the most elegant one at every occasion.'

'Master,' she sighed gratefully, 'it's just beautiful.'

It had never occurred to her that she would one day be on the end of his leash. Yet kneeling in front of him, staring at the collar, it seemed the most natural thing in the world, not to mention the most exciting. She felt the heat between her legs again.

'How do you feel about permanently wearing my collar, Elizabeth?' he asked.

Blushing, she replied sincerely, 'Honoured, master. Very honoured and proud indeed.'

Her perfect response pleased him. 'As you should be,' he mused, 'as you should be. Now, I shall snap the cameo back in,' he did so with deft fingers, 'and you will turn around so I can put your collar on you.' He lifted it, ready for her fitting.

She obeyed immediately, and then felt the cool gold lay against her skin as he placed it around her throat. His fingers worked a moment, and then were gone. The collar was in place. She turned back to face him and looked up.

'That is perfect, Elizabeth,' he said. 'You are perfect.'

She blushed, full of pride, feeling a lump in her throat.

'Now before I show you what's in the other box, go to the dresser and look at the cameo in my mirror.'

Puzzled, she said, 'Yes, master,' and standing up, moved across the bedroom to his dresser. She stared closely at the cameo reflected back at her, and let out a little cry.

'Master!' she exclaimed, running back to him. 'It looks like a beautiful girl kneeling obediently before a man!'

'Indeed it does. And every time you look in the mirror you'll be reminded of your place, won't you, my dear girl?'

She wanted to say that she did not need any reminding, but didn't. Instead she beamed happily, 'It's absolutely wonderful, master. Thank you so much.'

'On your knees, Elizabeth,' he ordered, his demeanour stern again. 'It is ust as well I designed it as I did. Evidently you do need reminding.'

She suddenly realised she was standing over him rather than kneeling before him, so she quickly dropped to her knees between his feet.

'Now then, this box,' he said, and opening the second slightly larger carton he removed another collar – but a very different collar to the first indeed.

'This is for training,' he said, and she stared at it. It was like a wide dog collar made of firm leather, with chrome rings in various places. It was fastened by a thin strap and buckle, sewn at each end.

'When you are in a training session the gold collar will come off, and this will be worn in its place,' he explained. 'As you can see,' he continued, lifting a woven black leather lead from the box, 'the leash is quite impressive, too.'

'Yes, master,' she concurred, her voice suddenly contrite and timid.

'Just as there are events to which you will wear your elegant gold collar, there will also be events to which you will wear this,' he said.

'Yes, master.'

'Place this collar and your two leashes in a safe place.

When I ask you to fetch them I will expect you to do so with all haste.'

'Yes, master.'

'It is official now, Elizabeth,' he stated. 'You are collared. I am your master.'

Flooded with emotion she did not trust herself to speak; instead she swallowed hard, willing away the lump forming in her throat.

'You think your journey has ended, but my sweet Elizabeth, it has only just begun. Put all your trust in me, and together we shall share many remarkable adventures.'

He leaned forward, touched his lips to hers, and savoured the soft, sweet, compliant kiss of submission.

All **Chimera** titles are available from your local bookshop or newsagent, or direct from our mail order department. Please send your order with your credit card details, a cheque or postal order (made payable to *Chimera Publishing Ltd*) to: **Chimera Publishing Ltd., Readers' Services, 22b Picton House, Hussar Court, Waterlooville, Hants, PO7 7SQ**. Or call our **24 hour telephone/fax credit card hotline: +44 (0)23 92 646062** (Visa, Mastercard, Switch, JCB and Solo only).

To order, send: Title, author, ISBN number and price for each book ordered, your full name and address, cheque or postal order for the total amount, and include the following for postage and packing:
UK and BFPO: £1.00 for the first book, and 50p for each additional book to a maximum of £3.50.
Overseas and Eire: £2.00 for the first book, £1.00 for the second and 50p for each additional book.

For a copy of our free catalogue please write to:

Chimera Publishing Ltd
Readers' Services
22b Picton House
Hussar Court
Waterlooville
Hants
PO7 7SQ

or email us at:
sales@chimerabooks.co.uk

or purchase from our range of superb titles at:
www.chimerabooks.co.uk